# The Lost Lagoon

The Lost Lagoon
© Copyright 2010 Reg Down

ISBN 13: 978-1453801963
ISBN 10: 1453801960

Lightly Press
regdown@hotmail.com

Third edition: 20 November 2013

# The Lost Lagoon

*in which is found*

## The Adam Tales

*Written and Illustrated*

*by*

## Reg Down

# ~ CONTENTS ~

*To Aran, Oisin and Isa*

\*\*\*

*How gloriously gleameth*
*All nature to me*
*How bright the sun beameth*
*How fresh is the lea!*

*White blossoms are bursting*
*The thickets among*
*And all the gay greenwood*
*Is ringing with song!*

*There's radiance and rapture*
*That naught can destroy,*
*O earth, in thy sunshine!*
*O heart, in thy joy!*

*from Goethe's 'May Song'*

# 1

## Tom Nutcracker meets the Iron Lady

Tom Nutcracker sat in the branches of an oak tree overlooking Running River. He loved this tree. He was certain that his favorite fairy, Tiptoes Lightly, lived here. He could feel her presence, and knew that she was somewhere hereabouts. She had golden hair, golden wings and a sky-blue dress. Once she'd told him that she lived inside an acorn, and he'd been searching for her house ever since. He peered here and there through the branches, but couldn't see any acorns.

"It's spring time," he thought, "and there aren't any acorns on the oak trees. So it should be simple to spot her house." But it wasn't easy finding a single acorn in a huge tree—even if this was Tiptoe's tree. Tom had looked in many trees, but he was sure this was the right one. It felt old and magical.

A strong breeze suddenly blew and the whole tree swayed. Tom held on tightly until the wind passed. He looked around. Behind him, the waxing moon hung pale in the sky over the Snowy Mountains. In front, Running River was full to the brim from melting snow and spring rains. Away in the west the afternoon sun glowed weakly and dark clouds were forming.

"Perhaps a storm is brewing," Tom thought.

"Yes, it is," said Tiptoes Lightly, suddenly appearing on a branch in front of him. "You'd better climb down."

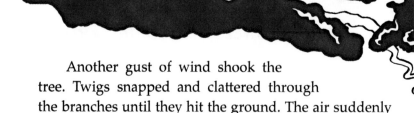

Another gust of wind shook the tree. Twigs snapped and clattered through the branches until they hit the ground. The air suddenly felt cooler.

"I was looking for your house," said Tom, happy that Tiptoes had turned up. Storm or no storm, he wanted to see her house for himself.

"There's no time," she said in a firm voice. "Climb down!"

Tom was shocked. Tiptoes had always seemed so sweet—but she was really as tough as nails.

"Get down, Tom," commanded Tiptoes, pointing to the ground. "Now!"

Tom climbed down—and not a moment too soon! The sky darkened and the sun fled. Three blasts of wind buffeted the tree. The last one was so strong it broke off a branch above his head. It crashed down, barely missing him, and smashed on the earth below.

Hardly had he reached the ground when lightning streaked across the sky—instantly followed by a thunderous roar. Tom ran! Quick as a rabbit he ran—but too late! Down poured the rain, soaking him from head to foot before he reached home. He crashed through the kitchen door, panting like a dog and dripping with water.

His father looked up from the kitchen table.

"I was wondering where you were," he said calmly.

No matter how dirty (or wet) Tom arrived home Farmer John never seemed to mind much.

"Better change your clothes," he grinned, pointing upstairs. "Looks like we're in for a storm."

# 2

## *Milking the Cows*

What a storm it was! The wind howled, lightning zigged and zagged across the sky, and rain came down in buckets. Farmer John put on his raincoat and trudged to the barn. As he closed the door the sounds of the storm died away and the warm, peaceful barn greeted him. June Berry was feeding the pony.

"Hi, Dad!" she called from Chiron's stall.

Farmer John went over and leaned on the half-door.

"Sure is stormy outside," he said, stroking Chiron's neck. "Tom came back as wet as a fish!"

June Berry laughed. "He wanted to find Tiptoes' acorn house. He's sure it's in the big oak tree down by Running River."

"It is, certainly," said Farmer John. "Though it's doubtful he'll find it."

June Berry looked at her father. She didn't know whether to take him seriously or not. He took fairies and gnomes for granted — but he also liked to pull her leg. June Berry decided to believe him.

"Why won't he find her house?" she asked.

"You can't find a fairy's house unless they show it to you," her dad replied.

June Berry nodded. That seemed like a good answer.

Farmer John went off to milk the cows while June Berry fed the hens. Afterwards she looked for eggs, but found only three.

Many hens were broody and sitting on their clutches. June Berry couldn't wait until the eggs hatched. She loved baby chicks, with their fluffy feathers and high-pitched peeping.

When he finished milking, Farmer John picked June Berry up, wrapped his raincoat around them both, and ran through the rain to the house.

They found Tom sitting in the living room beside the fire. He was looking at a book called 'The Adam Tales'. Tom couldn't read yet, but he knew a few words by sight and loved looking at pictures. Sometimes the pictures told better stories than the words.

"Can we read this book later?" he asked.

Farmer John nodded yes, and went to make supper.

When the dishes were washed and put away they sat on the sofa beside the fire. Lucy came too. He was their dog.* He lay down on Farmer John's feet and thumped his tail on the floor. Lucy loved Farmer John and followed him around whenever he could. For a while they listened to the wind moaning in the chimney and shaking the walls of the house. It felt good to be safe inside.

Tom handed 'The Adam Tales' to his dad. It was slim, with only a few pictures here and there. Farmer John had found it at the second-hand store in the village of Fairest Oaks. It was worn, and looked like it had been read many times. He opened it. The first chapter was called, *The Adam Child*.

* Yes, Lucy is a he. His full name is Luciano Amadeus Pavarotti von Nutcracker because he tries to sing along with the children. See *The Festival of Stones*.

# 3
## *The Adam Child*

Once, an angel child lived in the sky. He flew in and out amongst the stars and played with all the other angel children. One day he came upon the planet earth and found it beautiful.

"Oh, that planet looks so green and shining," he exclaimed, "with oceans of blue and billowing white clouds. I would like to live there."

So the angel child flew to his parents and asked to live on the earth.

"My child," they said, "you cannot live on the earth without a proper earth body. First you must make a pot of clay, and find the right animals. Fill the pot with water, put the animals inside, and jump into the pot yourself. Then say the magic word—and abracadabra!—you will have an earth body. But take care, dear child, to choose the right animals and say the right word."

So the angel child flew down to the earth. He wandered here, and he wandered there, till he came to a river. On the riverbank he found good clay to make a pot. It was golden brown, with a very fine grain, and as smooth as silk.

"This is perfect clay," he said to himself, and he fashioned a shapely pot with graceful, gently curving sides.

Then he gathered wood into a great pile, put the pot inside, and lit a fire. The flames crackled and burned merrily as the pot baked and hardened. When the fire had burned itself out and the pot had cooled, the angel child picked it up.

"This is a goodly pot," he said, "with no cracks or crooked parts. All I have to do now is find the right animals, pop them inside, say the magic word—and abracadabra!— I shall have an earth body to live in!"

He placed the pot high on the riverbank and off he went a-hunting. Over hill and over dale he journeyed till he came to a wide, grassland prairie. On the prairie he spied a bull grazing grass.

"Oh, what a fine animal!" he cried. "So heavy and strong! I shall take him to my pot." So he jumped onto the bull's back, and cried:

*"Mighty Bull! O Bull of mine!*
*Together we'll make a body divine!"*

The bull snorted and reared and bucked! He had never been ridden before! But the angel child just laughed. His body was made of light, and the bull could not throw him off no matter how hard he tried. The angel child spoke softly to the bull, and soon he stopped fighting and went wherever the child wished.

Off they traveled, over dale and over hill, until at last they reached the place where the pot had been left on the riverbank. But the pot was not in its place. It had tumbled down the bank and was lying on the shore. All around were the footprints of many animals.

"That's strange," thought the angel child. "I wonder what happened here?" and he put the pot back again, high on the riverbank.

He said to the bull: "Dear Bull, stay at this spot; I'll soon be back to fill my pot."

Off the angel child went a-hunting for the second time. Over field and over fen he traveled till he came to a forest. There he heard a mighty roar echoing through the trees. Closer and closer it came. Suddenly a lion appeared, walking fearlessly towards him!

"That is a fine animal," declared the angel child. "So brave and fierce!" He jumped upon the lion's back, and cried:

*"Majestic Lion! O Lion of mine!*
*Together we'll make a body divine!"*

O, how the lion roared! He had never been ridden before and he spun around and around in savage circles, snarling and spitting! But the angel child just laughed and spoke calmly to the lion until he was tamed. Then off they went, over fen and over field, back to the riverbank. But again the pot was not where it should be, and animal tracks were all around.

"I wonder where my pot went?" thought the child, looking all about. At last he found it under some bushes lying on its side.

"That's strange," he said. "I wonder who is moving this pot?" and he placed it back again on the riverbank.

Then he said to the lion: "Dear Lion, stay at this spot; I'll soon be back to fill my pot."

Away the angel child went a-hunting for the third time. Over veldt and over vale he journeyed till he came to a tall mountain. Up its craggy sides he clambered to the top. There he spied an eagle, perched on the highest peak.

"That is a fine animal!" he exclaimed. "So steely-eyed and fierce—and with such beautiful wings!" He leapt upon the eagle's back, and cried:

*"Fierce Eagle! O Eagle of mine!*
*Together we'll make a body divine!"*

Instantly the eagle took to the air. Up he swooped and down he dove; he twisted this way and that way, trying to throw the child off. But the angel child just laughed.

13

He was not afraid of flying; his body was made of light and he too had wings just like the eagle. Gently he spoke and gently he sang and soon the eagle was tamed. Then off they flew, high over vale and veldt, till they came to the riverbank.

But again the pot was not where it should be, and again animal tracks were all around. This time the angel child had to look high and low before he found the pot far down the river on the shores of an island.

"I wonder who is moving this pot?" he said to himself, and brought it back.

The angel child dipped the pot into the river and filled it with water. He called the eagle, the lion and the bull to him, and commanded:

"Into the pot my mighty bull!" and into the pot leapt the bull.

"Into the pot my fearless lion!" and into the pot sprang the lion.

"Into the pot my sharp-eyed eagle!" and into the pot plunged the eagle.

Last of all the angel child cried to himself: "Into the pot, you angel child!" and into the pot he leapt. He called out the magic word—and ABRACADABRA!—the pot began to shimmer and shake. It trembled and shook and shifted shape. A fine head appeared, with hair as golden as the lion's mane. Elegant arms emerged, with beautifully wrought hands and fingers. Two fine legs grew, with feet to run and jump and dance with.

At last the first human being stood on the earth. He was tall, upright and free, with the clear, piercing eyes of the eagle, the fearless heart of the lion and the great strength of the bull. He spoke, and the first word that came from his mouth was the magic word: 'I am'.

And if you had been there on the ancient riverbank, if you had looked into the first human eyes, you would have seen a fire burning within, and that fire was the light of the angels.

14

# 4

## *Tiptoes flies to Farmer John's*

Tiptoes sat in her acorn house high in the branches of the great oak tree. The storm raged around her and the house swung back and forth like a bell. Sometimes Tiptoes liked to be alone, but not tonight. The wind made her restless and she wanted company. Out into the storm she flew, darting this way and that to dodge the raindrops. Over the dark meadows she passed, heading for Farmer John's and the warm light streaming from his windows. At last she reached the back door, and making herself small, slipped through the keyhole.

She heard voices in the living room and went to look. Farmer John sat with Tom Nutcracker and June Berry in front of the fire. They had just finished reading from a book. On the back of the sofa, completely unnoticed, sat Pins and Needles, the house fairies. They'd been listening to the story too.

"Hello, Pins and Needles," said Tiptoes.

Pins and Needles waved. "Come sit with us," they called. "Farmer John just finished reading a chapter, but we're sure June Berry will ask for another one."

Tom Nutcracker stirred on the sofa. "Why was the pot moved?" he asked.

"It is strange," agreed June Berry. "There must be a reason."

Farmer John turned the page to see what the next chapter was about.

"What does it say?" asked Tom, peering intently at the words. He really wished he could read.

"The chapter is called: *Why the Pot was Moved the First Time*," said Farmer John, pointing to each word as he read.

"Read it, Dad—please!" begged June Berry. She knew if she begged hard enough that Farmer John would sometimes read two stories in one night.

"Okay," agreed Farmer John, smiling. He wanted to find out why the pot had moved just as much as his children. So they settled down again and he began to read.

# 5

# *Why the Pot was moved the first Time*

Once upon a very long time ago, just before the first human being lived on the earth, a beaver and his beaver wife lived beside a river. He was called Platey because his tail was extra flat, just like a plate, and she was called Pussy Cat because her fur was extra soft.

One day they found a pot high on the riverbank.

'What's this?' asked Platey, sniffing the pot. 'I've never seen such a thing. It must be magic!'

'Don't be silly,' said Pussy Cat his beaver wife. 'It's not magic! It's a good house lodge to live in!'

So they climbed inside and made themselves at home.

Not long afterwards a pair of ducks came waddling along. The daddy duck was called Bill because he had an extra fine bill, and the mama duck was called Ducky because she was always ducking her head under the water.

'Quack! Quack!' said Bill the duck. 'What's this funny thing? It looks like magic!'

'Don't be such a silly-Bill,' said Ducky duck. 'It's not magic! It's a nest to make our own!'

So they waddled inside and started to make eggs.

But the pot really was a magic pot! Whatever went inside got all mixed up together, and soon the pot began to shake. It shivered and shook so hard it fell over and tumbled down the riverbank. As it rolled, strange sounds came from inside; sounds like: oof! and poof!, eeek! and quack!

At last the pot stopped rolling and out came two strange creatures. Each had a duck's bill, but the fur and tail of a beaver, and they lived in the water and laid eggs.

Many animals gathered around and scratched their heads.

'What name shall we give this wonder?' asked the owl, hooting wisely.

'I know,' said the monkey, who thought himself very clever. 'We'll call them Deaverbucks. I think that's a good name!'

'No! No!' snorted the zebra, who did not like the monkey at all. 'That's a silly name for such complicated creatures. We should mix all their nicknames together.'

'Yes! Yes!' agreed the other animals—who didn't like the monkey either. 'That is a good idea!'

'Of course it's a good idea!' said the zebra, glad to have bettered the pesky monkey. 'We shall call them Plateybill-pussyduckys.'

And that is what they were called—or at least what they were called for a long, long time. But the name was so complicated that even the Plateybill-pussyduckys got mixed up and started to call themselves Pussybilled-plateyducks. Then, a thousand years later, they became confused again and called themselves Billyplated-duckypusses. And today, after much more confusion, they call themselves Duck-billed Platypuses and live in a wonderland called Australia. And if you don't believe me you can go Down Under and see some for yourself."

Tom was grinning. "Are there really such mixed up animals living in Australia?" he asked.

Farmer John nodded. "Yes," he said, "there are. They're funny looking creatures."

"Do they lay eggs too?" asked June Berry. She was fascinated.

Farmer John nodded again.

"That's weird!" she said.

Tom took the book from his dad and turned the page. He saw drawings of wild animals, and here and there a feather floating about. He tried to read the heading, but couldn't. He pulled his dad's sleeve and pointed to the title.

Farmer John looked at the page.

"It says: '*Why the Pot was Moved the Second Time*', or 'Why Tom Nutcracker and June Berry need to get ready for bed.'"

"It doesn't say that!" laughed June Berry, hitting her dad playfully.

"Well, maybe not," agreed Farmer John with a grin. "But it is time for little folk to brush their teeth and go to bed."

## 6

## *The Old Pine Tree*

Farmer John and his children weren't the only ones sitting out the storm at home. Deep in Farmer John's forest an old pine tree stood. Its roots were gnarled, its leaves were green, and its trunk was tall and tapered most elegantly. This tree was ancient and old, but hale and hearty—and it didn't mind if the wild wind blew. When a big storm came, it just dug its roots deeper into the ground, and cried:

*Blow, wind, and bluster,*
*Sleet and snow you muster!*
*But big I am and bold,*
*I love the rain and cold!*
*So blow, wind, and bluster,*
*I'll match your might and muster!*

And the wind huffed and puffed as hard as a hammer. It howled and lashed the forest with all its might—but the old pine tree just laughed. It dug its roots deeper into the ground, waved its branches in the air, and shook off its old needles and sent them whirling away in the wind.

20

"I wish this pine tree would dig its roots more carefully," grumped Pepper Pot, brushing dirt from his beard.

Pepper Pot is a gnome. He lives with his friend, Pine Cone, underneath the roots of the old pine tree. Every time the tree dug its roots deeper, bits and pieces of the ceiling broke off and pitter-pattered onto Pepper Pot's head. He was busy running around with a broom and dustpan, trying to keep things neat.

"Stop complaining and count your blessings," said Pine Cone. He was sitting in an armchair holding an umbrella over his head. "We have the best tree in the whole forest. Look at what happened to Red Berry and Green Berry last year."

Red Berry and Green Berry used to live under a yew tree close by. A winter storm had blown the tree over in the middle of the night. They'd woken up with no roof over their heads and the rain pouring down. Now they lived in a cedar tree close to Running River.

"That's true," agreed Pepper Pot, "we do have a good tree. But storms make such a mess—and this one's big. I wonder how long it will last?"

The storm lasted all night and into the next day. It howled and moaned and shook the air. Thunder giants stomped on top of the clouds and threw lightning bolts upon the mountains. But Pine Cone and Pepper Pot slept soundly that night and did not hear a thing. They'd put beeswax into their ears.

# 7

## *Farmer John sees Tiptoes' House*

All through the night the storm buffeted Farmer John's house. Windows rattled, curtains swung back and forth, and puffs of air blew in under the doors. Pins and Needles slept on the pin cushion in the sewing basket. When they're asleep, Pins looks just like a pin, and Needles looks just like a needle. If you saw them you'd think: 'There's a pin,' or 'There's a needle.' But they wouldn't be. And if you picked one of them up, you'd soon find that the pin or needle was missing, and no matter how hard you looked you'd never find it.

Tiptoes slept in the sewing basket too, on top of a piece of wool felt. If you saw her you'd exclaim: 'Oh, look! There's a fairy!'

In the morning Farmer John stepped out into the rain. It was pouring so heavily that he thought he'd better check his land. He trudged through the fields with his head down, the brim of his hat dripping water. Low lying land and hollows were feet deep in water and the river had risen to its brim.

"Running River is close to flooding," he said to himself, gazing around. But he wasn't worried; he sensed that the storm would end later in the day.

He wandered over to the great oak tree that Tom had climbed the day before and looked up. High above his head he saw a single acorn dancing to-and-fro in the wind. Farmer John smiled and chuckled to himself.

"I think I've found Tiptoes' house," he announced to Tom and June when he got home.

"You did!" they exclaimed. "Where?"

"In the great oak tree by Running River," he replied. "I saw it dancing in the wind."

"Can you climb up to it?" asked Tom, getting excited.

"Not on a wet and windy day," said Farmer John. "Perhaps on a sunny day with no wind you could get close to it—if you're careful, that is! It's pretty high!"

But Tom wasn't listening. He was already making plans to see Tiptoes' house for himself.

# 8

## Farmer John looks funny

It rained all morning and into the afternoon. Tom and June were going stir-crazy from being inside the whole day, so Farmer John sent them to the barn to muck out Chiron's stall and put down fresh hay for the calves. By the time they'd finished they were feeling better and ready for supper. On the way back to the house they found that the rain had stopped and the wind was chasing ragged clouds towards the Snowy Mountains.

That evening Farmer John read the next chapter of 'The Adam Tales'. Pins and Needles and Tiptoes Lightly came too. They decided to sit on Farmer John's head. He had a thick mat of hair which was very comfy to sit on. They'd just settled down when June Berry saw them and burst out laughing.

"The fairies are sitting on your head!" she exclaimed.

Farmer John looked puzzled and put his hand on top of his head—but the three fairies flitted out of the way. As soon as his hand was gone they settled onto his head again.

June Berry screeched with laughter and rolled around on the sofa. Tom looked annoyed. He didn't see the fairies and he couldn't see what was so funny. He wanted to hear the story.

"Stop it, June Berry!" he grumped. "Let's read the story!"

"But look, Tom!" she exclaimed. "*Look!*"

Tom looked—and suddenly he saw them! Pins and Needles and Tiptoes *were* sitting on his dad's head. They sat there looking very, very serious—far too serious to be taken seriously!

Tom's eyes widened, then he too rolled around the sofa, pointing at his dad's head and howling with laughter. By now the three fairies were grinning from ear to ear.

Farmer John didn't know what to think. He felt that something mischievous was afoot, but wasn't sure what it was. He stroked his hair a few times, but nothing was there. This made the children laugh even more because the fairies lifted off his head as his hand passed and then landed on his head again, just like a flock of birds.

"Okay! Okay!—Tiptoes and Company," he cried after a while, throwing his hands into the air and laughing. "I give up! But now it's time for the children to hear the story!"

So the three fairies sat on Farmer John's shoulder and the children settled down.

Farmer John opened 'The Adam Tales' and began to read.

"This chapter is called, "*Why the Pot was moved the second Time ~ or ~ Why the Animals didn't like the Monkey.*"

# 9

## *Why the Pot was moved the second Time*

### *~ or ~*

## *Why the Animals didn't like the Monkey*

Late one afternoon, when the world was still new and filled with wonders, two zebra came trotting along a riverbank. One was called Strips because he was a black zebra covered with white strips. And the other was called Stripes because she was a white zebra covered with black stripes. Strips and Stripes held their heads high and sniffed the air.

"We must be careful," said Strips. "There's a lion hereabouts. I can smell him."

"Yes," agreed Stripes, "I can smell him too. We must find a safe place for the night."

"I hope that pesky monkey is not around here either," said Strips. "He is such a pain in the …"

Just then a rotten mango came whizzing through the air and hit Strips on the rump.

"Hey!" he snorted, wheeling around.

"Hey to you!" jeered the monkey from high in a mango tree. "Get out of here!" and he began to pelt them with branches and fruit.

"Quick!" said Stripes. "You run around the mango tree that-a-way, and I'll run around the tree this-a-way," and off they galloped in opposite directions.

"You cowards!" screeched the monkey. "Stand still!"

He hurled mango after mango, branch after branch at them—but he always missed because he was turning round and round in the tree, his eyes dazzled by the zebra's stripes. Soon he was so dizzy that his head began to spin, and down from the tree he tumbled. Bouncing from branch to branch, jabbering and flailing wildly with his arms, he hit the ground with a loud thump and sent a cloud of dust billowing into the air.

In an instant Strips and Stripes galloped over to teach the monkey a lesson.

"Take that!" neighed Strips, lashing out with his hind legs.

"And this!" neighed Stripes, rearing up and striking hard with her forelegs.

But the monkey was too quick. He dodged their blows and took off across the veldt with the zebra pounding after him.

"Yea!" cried a herd of giraffe, joining in the chase. "Get the monkey!" They had been watching all the fuss from high on the ends of their long necks. They didn't like the monkey either because he threw rotten fruit at them whenever they tried to eat the leaves from his tree.

"Yea!" cried a flock of ostriches, also joining in the chase. "Get the monkey!" They didn't like the monkey at all because he stole their eggs or broke them just for fun.

The monkey darted this way and that, avoiding their kicks and pecks. What a to-do there was, with dust flying, giraffes snorting, zebra neighing, ostrich feathers floating hither and thither through the air, and the monkey howling and yammering! At one point the monkey became so desperate he leapt upon Stripe's back and hung on for dear life. Across the plain they raced, the ostriches chasing after them and pecking furiously at the monkey, until Stripes, bucking and heaving, threw him off and the chase continued.

Round and round, here and there they ran till they came to the pot sitting on the riverbank. The desperate monkey grabbed the pot and hurled it with all his might at a giraffe. It missed its mark, but through the air it sailed and landed in some bushes where the lion was taking his afternoon nap. The pot hit him squarely on the head.

"ROAR!" roared the lion angrily, his mighty voice shaking the air!

For an instant everyone froze.

"LION!" they all shouted at once, and took off as if their life depended on it—which it did!

And that is why the pot was not in its proper place the second time. And also why we still talk about how horrible it is 'to have a monkey on our back'. It was such a terrible experience for poor Stripes, that to this day not a single zebra will talk about it. If you don't believe me, you can ask a zebra yourself. Then you'll see how he stands there and refuses to say a word.

Farmer John closed the book.

"I bet I know what the next chapter is called," said Tom.

"I bet I know too," chimed in June Berry. "It'll be called: *Why the Pot was moved the third Time.*"

Tom nodded his head in agreement—and so did Pins and Needles and Tiptoes Lightly.

For a while they sat and listened to the sounds of the night. It was quiet and calm. From far away on Running River they heard the frogs beginning their evening chorus.

"Sounds like the storm has blown itself out," said Farmer John.

# 10

# *The Frogs of Soggy Mire*

It was evening and Pine Cone and Pepper Pot were wandering by the edge of Soggy Mire. The heavy rains from the storm had filled the mire to the brim. Scraggly trees and bushes sat with their roots in water, and all around the skirts of the mire the ground was wet and spongy.

The gnomes jumped from grassy tussock to grassy tussock, trying to keep their feet dry. At last they reached a tree which had fallen into the mire from the edge of the forest many years ago. Its bark had peeled off and now its trunk was smooth and silvery-grey. The gnomes ran out along the tree as far as they could go and stood by the water's edge. It was hazy, and an orange sun slanted through the forest trees behind them. All around, birds chirped and insects buzzed in the golden air.

Slowly the day closed. The almost full moon came riding over the mire and the frogs began to sing. Some frogs made deep croaking sounds, others sang as beautifully as birds. They sang about many things: how delicious the flies were, how yummy bugs and slugs tasted, and how the eyes of the lady frogs glistened like precious jewels.

After a while Pine Cone heard the frogs change their chorus. Five croaks were followed by a pause: ribbet~ribbet~ribbet~ribbet~ribbet … then five croaks again, and again.

A song was passing from frog to frog through the mire until the air was filled with only one melody.

"What are they saying?" asked Pepper Pot.

"I think they're singing about a lagoon," said Pine Cone. "Listen."

Sure enough, the frogs were singing a strange tune about a Lost Lagoon:

> *"Lost Lagoon is back again this almost …*
> *Moon full night that's mirrored in the sleeping …*
> *Waters still as silvered glass that's rarely …*
> *Gazed in by the moonlight's mystery waking …"*

"I've heard of the Lost Lagoon," said Pepper Pot. "It only comes when Running River is in full flood."

They listened as the frogs continued singing:

> *"We the frogs divine her by the waters …*
> *Lifting like our voices in the running …*
> *River full in flood-tide from the raindrops …*
> *Falling on the mountains steeply rising …*
>
> *Years have passed since Lost Lagoon was deeply …*
> *Hidden from the world beneath the arching …*
> *Branches great of trees that tower over …*
> *All that wish to find her beauty hiding …"*

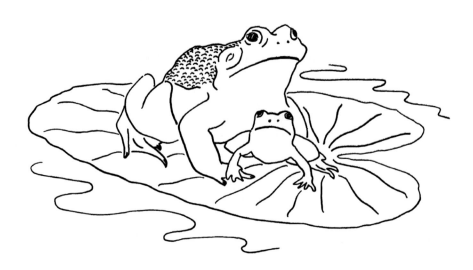

"That's right," said Pine Cone. "I've heard that the Lost Lagoon is a magical place. It's hidden beneath huge oak trees. It dries up so quickly that people who have seen it and want to go back again can never find it. That's why it's called the Lost Lagoon."

"Let's see if we can find it for ourselves," said Pepper Pot. "It sounds beautiful!"

Pine Cone bobbed his head up and down enthusiastically. "Yes!" he agreed. "Let's go tomorrow."

Then they stood for a while longer, listening to the frogs singing 'The Song of the Lost Lagoon' until it faded away into the distance.

*"Why the world from her is hidden until ...*
*Rain and moon and rising river running ...*
*Flood her full no human knows for certain ...*
*Knowing such as we the frogs are singing ..."*

At last the song faded away and all the gnomes heard were the big frogs deeply croaking, and the middle sized frogs calling, '*rib-bet, rib-bit*', and the little frogs chirping, '*peep-peep, go to sleep ... peep-peep, go to sleep*'.

# 11

## *Tiptoes flies Home*

Tiptoes said goodbye to Pins and Needles and flew out the keyhole into the night. The air was damp and a few clouds hung in the sky. The almost full moon floated over the Snowy Mountains in the east, its round face hazy from the misty air.

"It's going to be full moon tomorrow night," said Tiptoes to herself. She always felt a small, rising excitement inside her when the moon was waxing full.

Over the fields she flew, sometimes letting herself be caught by the gentle night breeze which twirled her around. Below her, Running River had burst its banks in many places and flowed out into the fields. Whole lakes had suddenly appeared on the landscape.

"I must visit Greenleaf the Sailor tomorrow," she thought. "His new spring boat is sure to be ready by now. This will be an exciting time to sail with him."

Then she flew to her acorn house dangling all alone by its slim stem high in the branches of the great oak tree.

In the night Tiptoes awoke. She listened. Running River was singing her flood-song. She sang of all the fields she'd swamped, all the mires she'd flooded, and how her swollen waters were sweeping down to the sea. There were many voices in her singing, many tales, like threads in a tapestry. One thread sounded like silver, a silver thread seldom heard but now reappearing. Over and over Tiptoes heard its voice: '*Lost Lagoon is back again … because of rain … because of rain.*'

Then she closed her eyes and fell deep asleep.

# 12

## *Pepper Pot's Pancakes*

Early in the morning a fresh spring wind sprung up. It swept the clouds and morning fog away and let the sun shine brightly through Pine Cone and Pepper Pot's window.

"Good morning, Gnomes," called the sun. "Time to wake up and clean the house."

Pine Cone and Pepper Pot yawned and stretched. They unwrapped their beards from around their heads (in case you don't know, gnomes sleep with their beards around their heads) and pulled on their bright red boots. Then they put on their pointy caps and cleaned the house. They sang as they worked:

> *"Sweep, sweep, sweep the floor,*
> *Toss the dirt out the door!*
> *Clean the tables and the chairs,*
> *Chase the bugs from under the stairs!"*

Soon the house was spic-and-span and looked fresh and clean.

"I'm hungry!" said Pine Cone.

"I'm not hungry!" said Pepper Pot. "I'm starving! I'm going to make pancakes," and he marched into the kitchen.

He lit the fire, pulled out a mixing bowl and started to mix the batter. He chanted his recipe as he worked:

> *"One bag of sugar,*
> *Or as much as you please,*
> *Ten shakes of pepper*
> *To make us all sneeze!"*

"Don't put in so much pepper!" called Pine Cone from the living room. "It makes me sneeze all morning!"

"Okay!" replied Pepper Pot, and he shook in nine shakes of pepper instead of ten. Then he continued:

> *"One pound of flour,*
> *And two sticks of butter,*
> *Three cups of yoghurt,*
> *And shake in more pepper."*

"Stop with the pepper, Pepper Pot!" shouted Pine Cone. "You'll blow my nose off!"

"Okay! Okay!" cried Pepper Pot, giving the pepper pot a last good shake.

> *"One dozen eggs,*
> *And mix till arm is sore;*
> *Fire up the frying pan*
> *And in the batter pour."*

"Are those pancakes ready yet?" called Pine Cone. His tummy was growling.

"Almost ready," said Pepper Pot. "I'm just laying the table."

Pepper Pot put two plates on the table, and set a knife and fork neatly next to each one. In the center of the table he placed a jug of maple syrup and a platter of butter.

"All ready," he called to Pine Cone, and they sat down together.

Pine Cone said grace:

> *"Bless this breakfast,*
> *And bless Pepper Pot;*
> *I hope he didn't use*
> *His namesake a lot!"*

"Amen!" said Pepper Pot, taking his first bite.

"Me too," agreed Pine Cone, and he wolfed down a whole pancake in no time flat.

Then he began to sneeze: "Achoo! ACHoo! ACH O

O

O

O

O

O

O

O

O

O

O

o!"

# 13

## *Muffin Making*

"Whoosh! Whoosh!" went the spring wind in the morning, huffing and puffing through the great oak tree.

"Whirl and twirl," laughed the leaves as they fluttered and shook.

"Snap and crackle," popped the twigs when they broke loose and spun through the air.

But Tiptoes' house hung on tight. The big storm hadn't shaken her little house free and this fresh spring wind certainly wouldn't blow it off! All it could do was chase the last clouds away over the Snowy Mountains.

Tiptoes laughed and called to the wind:

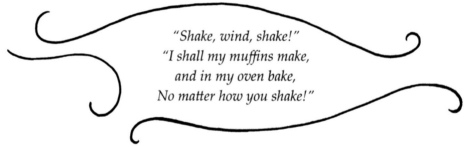

*"Shake, wind, shake!"*
*"I shall my muffins make,*
*and in my oven bake,*
*No matter how you shake!"*

It was early morning, so early that the stars were still shining brightly. Tiptoes was making muffins. She had decided to take Jeremy Mouse with her to visit Greenleaf the Sailor.

Greenleaf lived by Running River next to the old willow tree. Tiptoes knew he'd been making his new boat for the year. It was called, Little-Leaf: Number One Thousand, Six Hundred and Seventy-Two. That's how many years Greenleaf had been making leaf boats—ever since he was a boy elf. Not that Greenleaf looked old. He looked as young as a fresh spring leaf, even younger. Always. Except when you looked in his eyes and saw how many twinkles they held. That's how you knew he was very old. He had many merry adventures to tell (and some dangerous ones too), one for each shiny sparkle in his eyes.

"Whoosh! Whoosh!" sighed the wind again, rocking Tiptoes' house back and forth.

"This wind is blowing in from the sea," thought Tiptoes to herself. "I can smell the sea salt and feel the waves crashing on the shore."

Tiptoes opened her oven door and peeked inside. The muffins were done, all twelve of them, each one different: a blueberry one, an apple one, a strawberry one, even a muffin called Mouse's Tail. It was made from maple syrup and shredded carrots. Skinny pieces of carrot stuck out here and there and Jeremy Mouse had called it 'Mouse's Tail' just for fun.

"Whoosh! Whoosh!" blew the wind once more, making the acorn house spin round and round.

"Oh, Wind," called Tiptoes, getting exasperated. "Stop now! Enough whooshing and swooshing—you've been at it for too long!"

And the wind stopped blowing and became as still as a mouse—or at least as still as Jeremy Mouse. He was sound asleep in bed underneath the roots of the great oak tree.

"Thank you," said Tiptoes to the wind, and took the muffins out of the oven.

# 14

## *Jeremy Mouse is woken*

"Jeremy Mouse! Jeremy Mouse!" called Tiptoes, knocking at his door. "Time to get your tail out of bed!"

Jeremy Mouse doesn't like rain. He'd gone to bed when the storm came and slept for almost two days. Tiptoes heard the pitter-patter of mouse's feet. The door opened and a nose with sleepy whiskers peeked out.

"What time is it?" asked Jeremy Mouse, yawning. "The sun isn't even up yet!"

"It's time to get up!" replied Tiptoes, cheerfully flapping her golden wings. "Let's go sailing with Greenleaf. I want to see his new boat and find the Lost Lagoon. We have to get going."

Jeremy Mouse nodded and rubbed his eyes. He was used to Tiptoes hauling him off for an adventure, but this was a little early. He sniffed the air. "But there's no wind," he said hopefully. "Perhaps I should sleep until the wind comes. Then we can go sailing."

"Don't be silly," replied Tiptoes. "If we need the wind I can call it. I only told it to be quiet for a while. And besides, Greenleaf doesn't need wind for sailing."

Jeremy Mouse sniffed the air again. "Muffins!" he exclaimed. "I smell muffins! Did you make Mouse's Tail?"

"Yes, of course," said Tiptoes, nodding her pretty head up and down. "But the muffins are for later. Now brush your fur and wash your whiskers. We're late!"

# 15

## *Greenleaf the Sailor*
## *the*
## *Leaf Boat Maker*

Greenleaf the Sailor lives on the banks of Running River. His house is made of leaves and twigs cleverly put together. It has one door, two windows and a roof. From the door a pebble path meanders down to the water's edge.

"Greenleaf! Greenleaf!" called Tiptoes.

"Greenleaf! Greenleaf!" called Jeremy Mouse. He was excited about sailing with Greenleaf—he'd never done that before.

"Where's his house?" asked Jeremy Mouse, looking around. "I never can see it."

"Right in front of you," replied Tiptoes, pointing.

Jeremy Mouse looked really hard. It wasn't easy to see Greenleaf's house. On the outside it looked just like all the other leaves lying on the ground.

"Follow the pebbles," said Tiptoes. "Then you'll find it."

Jeremy Mouse looked for the pebble path. After a moment he found it—little flat pebbles poking out here and there amongst the leaves. He scampered up the path.

"Greenleaf! Greenleaf!" called Jeremy Mouse. "We've come for a visit!"

Out of his house came an elf. His clothes looked like leaves, his hat looked like a leaf, even his green shoes looked like two tiny leaves. He was very neat and tidy.

39

"Good morning, Jeremy Mouse," said Greenleaf with a smile. As he spoke sparkles of friendliness twinkled out of his eyes. "What are you doing here so early in the morning?"

"Tiptoes says you might take us sailing. She's talking about a secret place called the Lost Lagoon and wants to see if you can find it. She's also made muffins!"

"I see," said Greenleaf, nodding. "I was thinking of going to the Lost Lagoon myself. It's been ages since she's appeared and you never know when she'll come back again. But Jeremy Mouse, do you really want to go sailing? I've never had a mouse in my boat before."

Jeremy Mouse nodded his head up and down. He liked Greenleaf, and he did want to go sailing—especially with muffins to eat.

Greenleaf led the way down the pebble path to the river's edge. There, floating lightly on the water, was his new boat, Little-Leaf: Number One Thousand, Six Hundred and Seventy Two.

"She's beautiful!" exclaimed Jeremy Mouse, jumping up and down. "How did you make her so perfectly?"

"I sang her," said Greenleaf.

"Sang her!" exclaimed Jeremy Mouse, surprised.

"Yes," said Greenleaf. "Every spring I sing a new boat. First I choose a tree and find a bud about to burst. Then I sit on the branch beside it and sing."

"That's right," said Tiptoes, nodding her head. She had often heard Greenleaf singing a boat in springtime. "Day and night he sings, sometimes softly, sometimes loudly, sometimes quickly and sometimes slowly. Bit by bit the bud opens and the leaf listens to his song. This makes the leaf dance. It dances slowly, as slow as leaves grow. But songs and dances have shapes, and bit by bit the leaf takes shape until the boat is made."

"And after it's made," added Greenleaf, "I go to the bees to gather wax. Then I wax the boat to make it watertight."

Greenleaf was a master boat maker. All of his boats were beautiful, with curved prows that stood out proudly.

"But where's the sail?" asked Jeremy Mouse.

"Greenleaf doesn't need one," said Tiptoes with a twinkle in her eye.

Jeremy Mouse scratched his head. He was puzzled.

"But how can you go sailing without a sail?" he asked.

"You'll see," said Tiptoes, "but first you have to get into the boat."

So Jeremy Mouse did.

# 16

## *The Rainbow*

Jeremy Mouse climbed into Greenleaf's boat. He sat in the middle because that seemed the safest place for a mouse. Then in jumped Tiptoes; she sat at the back. Last of all came Greenleaf who stood by the prow. Greenleaf's boat didn't have a sail because it didn't need one. All he had to do was call out, "Sail, little boat, sail!" and off the little boat went.

At first they wound slowly in and out between the reeds by the shore. Jeremy Mouse looked into the water. It was brown with silt, and Running River was so full that some reeds were completely submerged. The flowing water gurgled quietly and the reeds swayed back and forth in the current. They hissed softly when they rubbed against each other.

The morning sun shone low through the trees and mist covered the river. Now and then a fish jumped out of the water with a splash. Greenleaf listened. He loved being on the water when everything was so quiet.

They saw a mist fairy twirling round and round over the river, one toe touching the water and making tiny whirlpools. Then she lifted into the air and spun away.

The little boat glided out into the current and Running River tried to carry it downstream, but Greenleaf didn't let that happen. He sang:

> *"Little boat, turn your head,*
> *Up the river go instead!"*

Up the river the leaf boat bobbed, skimming lightly over the waves. They passed through the forest on Farmer John's land where the trees hung over the water. Jeremy Mouse looked to the shore and saw a fox on the riverbank gazing at them with knowing eyes. Then the fox turned and loped away on his long legs.

The forest ended, and the morning mist lightened and lifted from the water. The sun cleared the trees behind them and a rainbow appeared in the sky. It shimmered and sparkled in the air before them and spanned the river from bank to bank.

Greenleaf suddenly called out loudly and the leaf boat sprang forward. It sailed right through the rainbow's arch.

Jeremy Mouse gasped and Tiptoes clapped her hands with joy. The world had changed into a sea of flowing color. There before them hovered a rainbow angel with wings as wide and blue as the sky!

# 17

# *The Rainbow Angel's Tale*

Every rainbow has an angel. She lives on the other side of the rainbow's arch. When you go through the arch there she is!

"Good morning, little sailors," said the angel.

Actually, she didn't really say, 'Good morning'. She changed her colors so that they *saw* a good morning and knew what she meant.

"What can I give you?" she asked, her question full of fresh green and yellow, with hovering gray-violet tinges.

Jeremy Mouse couldn't say a word. His mouth was stuck open and wouldn't move.

"A color tale!" replied Tiptoes, a big smile on her face. She loved rainbow angels.

"Yes! Yes!" echoed Greenleaf. "Tell us a color tale!"

The angel smiled a smile full of sunny yellow and pink, with touches of bright green. She nodded her head and began her tale.

"There was once a golden star living high in the bluest of skies."

As soon as the angel spoke, Jeremy Mouse found himself in the bluest of blue skies with a radiant, golden star shining at the center. He was inside the star and inside the blue sky all at the same time!

"For many years the star was as happy as a lark, and shone every day of every year as brightly as can be.

But at last it thought to itself: 'Why am I always shining from the center and the sky is always out there blueing all around me?'

So the golden star asked the blue sky: 'Dear Blue Heavens, may I send my golden heart into your blueness to see what becomes?'

And the blue sky answered: 'Yes, of course, dear Most Golden Star, you are welcome to send out your heart to see what becomes.'

44

So the golden star shone its heart out and the blue heavens wrapped around it. And what do you think happened? Ah! The most radiant of gems! A planet called Earth, with green grass and green trees growing all over it. No one had ever seen such a thing and they wondered and wondered."

Jeremy Mouse saw all this in front of his eyes. The angel had told her story in colors so alive it seemed that he'd never seen colors before.

"Is that the end?" he asked the angel. "Couldn't you tell us more?"

Tiptoes gave Jeremy Mouse a dig in the ribs, as if to say he shouldn't ask angels such questions.

But Jeremy Mouse ignored her. "It's a beautiful story," he said. Please tell us more."

The Rainbow Angel nodded her head, shifting her colors in such a way that Jeremy Mouse knew she was pleased he'd asked.

"Well," the angel continued, "the golden star was so happy with the green earth that it sent down sun-sparks in summer time to become sunny sunflowers and golden buttercups and flitting butterflies — even yellow butter to spread on toasty toast at breakfast time. And the sky was so pleased with the world that it laid its gentle blue mantle on the seas and lakes, and in the eyes of blue-eyed children and forget-me-nots and blue bells.

"And Tiptoes' dress," added Jeremy Mouse. "You can't forget that!"

"And Tiptoes' beautiful sky-blue dress too," agreed the angel with a nod. "But, in winter time," she said, rapidly changing hues, "when all is cold and dreary, Mother Mary wraps her lovely blue mantle around the star that is her son. She holds him so gently that her love shines with the greenest of greens in her golden son's heart."

Then the angel stretched her wings as huge and blue as the sky, and vanished.

"Hey! Where'd she go?" exclaimed Jeremy Mouse. "And where's the rainbow?"

"When the angel goes, the rainbow goes too," said Greenleaf.

"She was beautiful," sighed Jeremy Mouse. "Even more beautiful than the rainbow."

"Yes," agreed Tiptoes. "We were lucky to be in the right place at the right time—and to have such a fine boatman as Greenleaf the Sailor to sail us through the rainbow's arch."

# 18

## *Pine Cone and Pepper Pot meet Mr. Fox*

Pine Cone and Pepper Pot finished breakfast and washed the dishes.

"I think I'll make traveling biscuits," said Pine Cone. "It might take us a long time to find the Lost Lagoon."

"That's a good idea," agreed Pepper Pot. "I'll help."

So they baked traveling biscuits from oats and raisins and sunflower seeds (but no pepper) and wrapped them in clean handkerchiefs.

"That should keep us from getting too hungry," said Pine Cone as he pulled on his wandering boots.

"I hope so," replied Pepper Pot doubtfully. "If we meet Jeremy Mouse we'll have to share them. Then there won't be very many at all."

Before they left, Pine Cone took out two small velvet bags and placed a tiny silver bucket and silver feather into each one. He put one into his pocket and gave the other to Pepper Pot. Out the door they strode into the forest. They rambled down their favorite path towards Running River. It meandered through old trees with gnarly roots and branches hung with Old Man's Beard. Then it wound amongst young trees decked out with fresh spring leaves and sporting barks of many hues.

At last they reached the riverbank. There they found silvery-white dew lying on the grass. The morning sun shone on the dew drops and they sparkled with small, colorful lights. Pine Cone got down on his hunkers and looked at one. He tilted his head from side to side and rocked back and forth on his feet.

"Pepper Pot," he called. "Come look! There's a rainbow inside this dewdrop."

Pepper Pot came over and looked carefully.

"There is a tiny rainbow inside!" he exclaimed. "And look! There's another in this dewdrop over here!"

"And one over here!" called Pine Cone, searching around.

"And one here too!" shouted Pepper Pot.

Everywhere they looked, tiny rainbows sparkled inside the dewdrops.

"Perhaps that's how rainbows get their colors," said Pine Cone. "From all the drops of rain."

"Yes," agreed Pepper Pot. "I think so too. The rainbow angel says: 'Hey! You! Little drop over there! You be a green drop. And you over there—you be a red drop. Quick as a wink all the drops make a rainbow!'"

Pine Cone nodded in agreement and the gnomes looked at each other in wonder and surprise.

Suddenly a mob of crows started to flap their wings and caw loudly in the trees.

"Why are they making such a racket?" wondered Pepper Pot, looking up.

"Because of me," said Mr. Fox, trotting out of the forest.

Mr. Fox was a lovely shade of browny-red with a dark tip on the end of his tail. He looked clever, even a little sly.

"Those pesky crows set up such a racket whenever I'm around," grumped Mr. Fox. "I wish they'd mind their own business."

Pine Cone and Pepper Pot nodded understandingly. Crows could be pesky creatures—though the real reason they were crowing was to warn all the little animals that Mr. Fox was around and might be looking for something to eat.

"We're off to find the Lost Lagoon," said Pine Cone, changing the subject.

"We heard the frogs singing about it last night," added Pepper Pot. "They said that it's back again and we've never seen it."

"I heard the frogs too," said Mr. Fox. "But you're not the only ones looking for the Lost Lagoon. I just saw Greenleaf the Sailor sailing by in his new boat. Tiptoes and Jeremy Mouse were with him."

"Where were they?" asked Pine Cone, getting excited. "Perhaps we can get a ride too."

"Up the river that-a-way," replied Mr. Fox, pointing with his nose. "If you hurry you might catch up with them."

"Thank you, Mr. Fox!" called Pine Cone and Pepper Pot, and off they ran along the riverbank.

# 19

## *The Vanishing*

Pine Cone and Pepper Pot raced along the riverbank. They dodged roots and branches and wove in and out between reeds and rushes. Once or twice they leapt high into the air to clear a log. They looked funny when they jumped because they held onto their caps with both hands to stop them from falling off.

After a while the riverbank rose and they ran onto a meadow. It was covered with short grass and thousands of bright yellow dandelions. They stopped and looked down on Running River. A most beautiful rainbow had appeared, arching from bank to bank. In front of the rainbow was a boat.

"There they are!" cried Pepper Pot, leaping up and down and pointing.

"Yoo-hoo! Tiptoes!" shouted Pine Cone, waving his arms.

"Yoo-hoo, Greenleaf!" shouted Pepper Pot, waving his hat in the air.

Greenleaf was standing at the prow and looking intently ahead. Jeremy Mouse and Tiptoes Lightly were staring ahead too. They were so intent that they didn't hear the gnomes calling.

"They don't hear us at all," said Pine Cone. "They're absorbed in the rainbow."

Suddenly Greenleaf called out loudly and the boat leaped forward at his word. Into the rainbow they sailed—and disappeared!

"Where did they go?" cried Pepper Pot in surprise.

"I don't know!" said Pine Cone, astonished.

The gnomes ran backwards and forwards along the meadow, but there was no sign of the leaf boat. Tiptoes, Jeremy Mouse and Greenleaf the Sailor had vanished completely!

# 20

# *The Reappearing*

Pine Cone and Pepper Pot were puzzled. They took off their hats and scratched their beards. They held hands, put their heads together, and sent a calling-thought to Tiptoes—but there was no reply.

"Where did they go?" wondered Pepper Pot.

"They just vanished into the rainbow!" said Pine Cone in amazement. "They're gone!"

The gnomes didn't know what to do except wait. So they found an old tree stump overlooking the river and waited. Now and then Pepper Pot chewed his beard. He was worried.

Then, as suddenly as they'd disappeared, the three sailors and their little boat reappeared in the exact same spot, as if no time had passed at all.

"There they are!" shouted Pepper Pot, jumping to his feet.

"Yoo-hoo! Yoo-hoo!" cried the gnomes as loudly as they could. "Yoo-hoo! Yoo-hoo!"

This time their shouts were heard. Tiptoes stood up in the boat and waved and Greenleaf sailed towards the shore. The gnomes jumped down from the tree stump and tumbled helter-skelter to the river's edge.

"Where did you go?" asked Pepper Pot excitedly. "You vanished into thin air!"

"We did?" said Jeremy Mouse, looking puzzled.

"Yes, you vanished completely!" said Pine Cone. "One minute you were there—then you sailed into the rainbow, and poof, you were gone!" and he snapped his fingers in the air. "We were worried!"

"We didn't feel like we vanished," said Tiptoes. "We saw the rainbow and Greenleaf sailed into it."

"We met the rainbow angel," added Jeremy Mouse. "She told us a story."

Pine Cone and Pepper Pot listened attentively as Jeremy Mouse retold the whole adventure.

"That's beautiful," said Pine Cone wistfully. "I wish I'd been there."

"Me too," said Pepper Pot.

Greenleaf stood quietly by. He had a knowing look in his eye. He knew that rainbows don't really belong on earth. When you go inside one then you're somewhere else—that's why they'd vanished.

"What are you two doing so far from home?" asked Tiptoes.

"We're looking for the Lost Lagoon," explained Pine Cone. "We heard the frogs singing about it in Soggy Mire last night. We wanted to see it for ourselves."

"That's where we're going too!" said Jeremy Mouse.

"We know," said Pepper Pot. "Mr. Fox told us."

Greenleaf helped the gnomes into the boat and off they sailed up Running River—and it wasn't long before Jeremy Mouse was munching on the traveling biscuits that the gnomes had made to keep from getting hungry.

# 21

## Little Leaf shows its Stuff

Greenleaf sang and spurred his boat up Running River. Mostly his songs were in Elfish and didn't make much sense to Jeremy Mouse—but suddenly Greenleaf sang something he did understand.

> *"Leap forward, Little Leaf,*
> *Number: One Thousand, Six Hundred and Seventy-Two—*
> *Let's show our sailor-mouse*
> *What a Greenleaf boat can do!"*

Over the waves the little boat leapt. Faster and faster it sped and Jeremy Mouse clapped his paws with glee—this was fun! Soon the boat was going so fast that it whizzed up a wave, flew into the air, and landed in the water with a splash.

"Whee!" shouted Tiptoes gleefully.

"Yee-haw!" shouted Pine Cone and Pepper Pot as if they were riding a wild horse.

"Eeek!" squeaked Jeremy Mouse who didn't like flying at all, not even in a boat.

In a few moments Jeremy Mouse began to look green.

"Slow down, Greenleaf," shouted Tiptoes, "or Jeremy Mouse will get sick. Then he won't be able to eat any muffins!"

Greenleaf laughed and sang a slowing-down song.

*"Whoa! Whoa! Little Leaf,*
*Number: One Thousand, Six Hundred and Seventy-Two!*
*A seasick sailor-mouse just won't do!"*

Instantly the boat slowed to a leisurely pace.

"Thank you, Greenleaf," said Jeremy Mouse. "But, oh dear!" he moaned, suddenly lying down, "my tummy feels funny."

"I'll help you feel better," said Tiptoes. She waved her hand over Jeremy Mouse's tummy and said a charm against seasickness:

*"Seasickness, seasickness,*
*Listen to me!*
*Come out of this tummy*
*Before I spell three:*
*T – H – R – E – E !"*

And sure enough, Jeremy stopped looking so green and turned a proper color for a mouse.

"I'm hungry," he said. "When can we eat our muffins?"

"When we find the Lost Lagoon," answered Tiptoes, laughing at how quickly Jeremy Mouse felt better.

"I'm sure that will take forever," grumped Jeremy Mouse. "It's probably not called the Lost Lagoon for nothing!"

# 22

## *The Oh-Oh! Tree*

Pine Cone and Pepper Pot peered ahead. They were keeping a sharp eye out for flotsam on Running River. It was swollen so high that huge branches, even whole trees, went floating past.

"How far is the Lost Lagoon?" asked Pine Cone.

"It's a ways yet," answered Greenleaf. "And it's hard to find. It comes so seldom that it never looks the same twice. And there's no proper channel to it either," he added. "Last time I had to look for ages before I found my way in."

On they sailed, following the river as it wandered back and forth through Farmer John's fields and into the wild lands beyond. They passed under a canopy of trees with dusky green leaves and came to sandy-brown bluffs dropping steeply into the water. At the highest point an oak tree stood half on and half off the bluff. It was completely upright and looked quite unconcerned, as if there was nothing wrong with dangling over the edge of a cliff! It had been standing in mid-air for many years and everyone expected it to fall over soon—but it never did. Tiptoes called it the 'Oh-Oh! Tree' because that's how she would feel if she was about to fall off a cliff.

They sailed around a bend in the river and the bluffs were lost from sight. A long, low island appeared. It had gravel shores dotted with scraggly bushes, and a slim meadow, covered with wildflowers, ran down the middle.

"Let's stop for elevenses," said Jeremy Mouse, hopefully. He was getting really peckish.

They pulled the leaf boat out of the water and made sure it was safe. Pine Cone unwrapped a traveling biscuit and shared it with everyone. Jeremy Mouse wanted more but Pine Cone told him they'd surely need some biscuits later.

Jeremy Mouse curled up on a warm rock for his after-snack nap. This was not a good idea because there were hawks hereabouts — but Pine Cone and Pepper Pot sat next to him and kept a sharp look out for danger. Greenleaf rested against a willow sapling and played his flute softly. The melody was wistful and sweet. It sounded like a journey, perhaps one that Greenleaf had taken a long time ago. Soon Jeremy Mouse was fast asleep and dreaming of hazelnuts and cheese.

# 23

# *The Toad*

Tiptoes wandered along the shore. She found a large, flat stone sticking out of the riverbank. It was covered with slimy moss and brown mud. A toad's head stuck out from the shadows underneath. He didn't look happy.

"What are you doing?" croaked the toad. "This is my rock and I live here."

"Just walking and exploring," replied Tiptoes. "It's a beautiful day."

The toad stared at Tiptoes with baleful eyes. "I don't like beautiful days," he grumped. "Beautiful days are bright; the sun hurts my eyes."

"Oh," said Tiptoes, looking disappointed. Tiptoes loved the sun, he was her father, and it hurt when someone did not like the sunlight.

"Shadows are nice too," she said at last, "especially on a hot day. It's wonderful to sit in the cool shade," and she sat down next to the toad.

The toad pulled back beneath the stone and glared at her.

"Are you a princess?" he asked.

"No," laughed Tiptoes. "I'm not a princess. I'm a fairy called Tiptoes Lightly! Why do you ask?"

"Princesses are dangerous!" croaked the toad. "Very dangerous!"

"Real princesses are beautiful," said Tiptoes. "Only false princesses are dangerous."

"I think both are dangerous," said the toad.

"Why?" asked Tiptoes.

"Because both are beautiful. When a beautiful princess comes close, we toads get uglier and uglier until we die."

"Hmm," said Tiptoes, pondering. "I'm not sure of that. Have you ever seen a princess?"

"No," said the toad.

"Then how do you know they're dangerous?"

"Because my mother told me. She told me what happened between the ugly toad and the princess."

"What did she say?" asked Tiptoes.

The toad stared at her for a long time, his golden eyes glistening in the shadows.

"I'll tell you," he said at last. "It's a short story. A very short story," and he cleared his throat with a deep 'rrrrrribbit'.

"Underneath a stone lived a toad. He was ugly, with warts on his back. He ate flies when he could, and slugs when he couldn't. He didn't much like anybody, and preferred to be alone. One day a princess came along and killed him with a look."

"That's it," said the toad. "I told you it was short."

Tiptoes sat for a while. "That is a complicated tale," she said at last. "You could think about it for a long time."

"Yes, you could," agreed the toad, "and I have. I think that princesses are dangerous."

"Well," said Tiptoes, "I will tell you another tale about a toad and a princess; then you will have two stories to think about."

This is the tale she told.

# 24

## *The Toad under the Stone*

Once upon a time, a large and very ugly toad lived beneath a stone near a castle. Every evening the toad plopped into the moat, and croaked: 'Ribbit-ribbit! Ribbit-ribbit!'

Within the castle lived a young and beautiful princess. She was as lovely as the sun and stars, and her hair shone like gold.

One day the princess went for a walk in the woods, and as she wandered she stubbed her toe on the toad's stone.

'Ow! Ow! Ow!' she cried, 'My poor toe!' and went limping back to the castle.

In her room she sat on a chair and wrapped her toe in a bandage. But as she was doing so, the toad came plip-plop, plip-plop up the stairs and stopped in front of her.

'Ribbit,' croaked the toad. 'I can make your toe better.'

'How can you do that?' asked the princess.

'Ribbit-ribbit,' answered the toad. 'I can kiss it.'

'Eeeeeyou!' squealed the princess. 'How gross!' And turning her head in disgust she told the ugly toad to go away.

That night, after she went to bed, her toe grew bigger and bigger. It swelled up until it was as big as a grapefruit.

In the morning her toe was very sore. So sore that all the princess could do was limp to her chair and sit down.

Before long the toad came plip-plop, plip-plop up the stairs. He hopped to the princess, and said: 'Ribbit! Ribbit! I can make your toe better.'

'How can you do that?' she asked, hoping the toad would give a different answer. But the toad replied in a croaky voice: 'I can kiss it— ribbit—I can kiss it.'

The princess turned her nose up into the air, and said: 'Eeeeeyou! How gross and disgusting! I definitely don't want that! Not from such an ugly toad as you!'

That night her toe got worse. It swelled until it could swell no more. It should have burst—but the end of her nose began to swell instead. It swelled until it was as large as a ripe tomato—and just as red!

In the morning she got out of bed and looked in the mirror.

'*Eeeeeyou!*' she cried when she saw how ugly she was. 'How gross and disgusting!'

She hobbled painfully to her chair, sat down, and waited. Soon the toad came plip-plop, plip-plop up the stairs and stopped in front of her.

'Ribbit! Ribbit!' croaked the toad. 'I can make your toe better.'

'How will you do that?' cried the princess in agony.

'Ribbit,' croaked the toad. 'I can kiss it. I can kiss it.'

This time the princess was glad to say 'yes' to the ugly toad, and he hopped over and kissed her toe. Instantly her toe was better. At the same moment, the toad vanished and a handsome prince appeared. It was not long before wedding bells were ringing from every church in the land, and they lived happily ever after."

When Tiptoes finished her story the toad didn't say a word. Tiptoes waited patiently.

"Do you think that toads really have princes hidden inside them?" asked the toad at last.

"This one did," said Tiptoes. "Perhaps you do too!"

The toad looked at her doubtfully.

"It will take a long time for my prince to come out into the world," he said at last.

"Perhaps," said Tiptoes, "but he's in there somewhere."

"Maybe," agreed the toad. He was less grumpy now. "But tell me, Tiptoes, what became of the ugly red swelling on the end of the princess's nose?"

"Well," said Tiptoes, "the swelling did go down, but not quite. For the rest of her life the beautiful princess had a pimple on the end of her nose, to remind her of how snotty she had been, once upon a time."

# 25

## *The Sun Hero*

Tiptoes wandered further along the shore. Sometimes she hopped from stone to stone, or stopped to gaze into the water. The sun was shining brightly in the sky and a gentle breeze wafted up the river and played with her golden hair. Tiptoes stopped and raised her arms to the sun.

"Thank you, Father Sun, for giving us light," she called.

"You're welcome, my little daughter," replied the Sun. "I see you've been talking to Mr. Toad-under-the-Stone. He never comes out if he can help it."

"That's right," said Tiptoes. "He says you are too bright."

"Perhaps I am," agreed the Sun. "But I can't stop shining because of folk who live in the shadows. Besides, if I didn't shine, there wouldn't be any shadows to live in—then what would Mr. Toad do?"

"That's true!" said Tiptoes. "I never thought of that. And there wouldn't be cool shade in summertime either. So I have to thank you, dear Father Sun, for the sunshine and the shade!"

Tiptoes walked onto the meadow running down the middle of the island and thought about sunlight and shadows. She looked at the bright orange poppies swaying in the breeze and their shadows dancing on the grass. Everywhere she looked she saw shadows, some dim and some dark, some warm and some cool. She was so busy looking around that she almost stepped on a grasshopper.

"Hey!" cried the grasshopper, jumping into the air.

"Eeek!" squealed Tiptoes, leaping aside.

"Watch where you're going, Madam Fairy!" said the grasshopper. "You almost stepped on me!"

"I'm sorry, Mr. Grasshopper. You were sitting so very still. I was thinking about the sun and didn't see you."

"The sun! The sun!" chirped the grasshopper. "I love the sun as well! He's my hero! Is he your hero too?"

"Yes," laughed Tiptoes. "I guess he is."

"Me too," sighed the grasshopper, looking lovingly up at the sun. "He's the biggest grasshopper in the whole wide world!"

Tiptoes smiled. "I'm not sure the sun is a grasshopper," she said, doubtfully crossing her arms. "How could he be a grasshopper?"

"Oh, he is a grasshopper! He is!" said the grasshopper enthusiastically. "He definitely is! Who has the biggest hop in the whole world? You answer me that, Madam Fairy with the Golden Wings. Who do you think that hopper is? The sun of course! He's the biggest hopper! The most magnificent and most biggest hopper of all! He's so huge that he hops into the sky every morning and lands on the other side of the earth at night. Only a great grasshopper could do that!"

Tiptoes laughed. "Maybe you're right," she agreed.

"Of course I'm right!" said the grasshopper, really getting excited. "I have thought about it for a long time. What else could the sun be? I've even made a song about him. Do you want to hear it?"

"Yes," said Tiptoes. "That would be lovely."

So the grasshopper rubbed his legs against his wings until he had the right note. Then he cleared his throat, did a little bow towards Tiptoes, and said: "This is the Song of Hop-o-lay Grasshopper—that's me, of course—and his Hero, the Great Grasshopper Sun in the Sky."

This is what he sang:

"Hop-o-lay Grasshopper
hid in the hay,
humming and dreaming
and singing Ho-hey!
Ho-diddle-dee hiddle-dee
hiddle-hum-hey!
The sun is his hero,
he hops o'er the day!'

O hark to the lark
as he soars up on high!
Hallelujah Moon Mother
as you rush o'er the sky!
All Hail to the Great God,
Ho-diddle hum-hey!
The sun is his hero
he hops o'er the day!

Hop-o-lay Grasshopper
sings when it's hot,
he hums in the heat,
and leaps when he's caught!
He's happy at Halloween
behind a warm stove,
and hushed in winter
when the hoary ground's froze.
For the sun is his hero,
Hey-diddle hum-hey!
He leaps up in morning
and hops o'er the day!"

64

"Yea!" cried Tiptoes, clapping her hands. "That's a wonderful song! Did you really make it up?"

"I did," said the grasshopper, blushing just a little bit. "I'm quite famous in this meadow for my singing."

"So you should be," said Tiptoes, patting him on the back. But Tiptoes had forgotten that you should never, ever pat a grasshopper on its back—unless you want it to jump.

"Oi!" cried the grasshopper, exploding into the air.

"Yikes!" gasped Tiptoes, falling backwards.

"Bye, little fairy," called Hop-o-lay … bounce … bounce … bouncing away over the meadow.

"Bye!" called Tiptoes, waving after him. "Nice to meet you!"

But Hop-o-lay Grasshopper was already far, far away, leaping lightly into the air and telling everyone he met that the sun was his best and hoppiest hero.

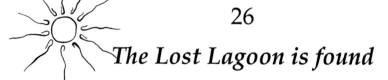

# 26
## *The Lost Lagoon is found*

Greenleaf peered intently ahead. They had been sailing up river for a long time since leaving the island and it was well past lunch. They'd come to a wild stretch of land, heavily flooded over. Running River had broken up into many channels big and small, and they'd still not found the one leading to the Lost Lagoon.

"I'm hungry," said Jeremy Mouse, holding his tummy and looking at the sun. "It must be getting late. See how high the sun is."

The sun smiled back at Jeremy Mouse, but didn't say a word.

"I'd love just a little nibble of a muffin?" he begged Tiptoes.

But Tiptoes shook her head and kept looking at the shore.

"Can't I have a biscuit crumb?" he asked Pine Cone, but Pine Cone shook his head too.

"How about you, Greenleaf?" asked Jeremy Mouse hopefully. "You're the captain of this boat, you're the real boss. Can't I have a smidgen of something?"

Greenleaf didn't say anything. He just kept humming to himself and searching ahead with his intense eyes.

"Barley brats!" muttered Jeremy Mouse. "Don't ever go sailing with fairies. They never seem to be hungry."

Greenleaf tried channel after channel, but quickly found that each one led nowhere.

"Tiptoes, why don't you fly into the air and find the silly Lagoon?" said Jeremy Mouse. He was getting impatient.

"She could try," said Greenleaf, "but you can't see the Lost Lagoon from the air. It's hidden."

Jeremy Mouse leaned over the side of the boat and gazed into the water. He saw his grumpy reflection shifting shape and grinning back at him. Then, through his reflection, he saw another face. It was a woman's face, with friendly, greeny-blue eyes, and long, silvery hair that waved languidly to and fro in the current. The water-woman smiled at him, and reaching out her arm, pointed towards a clump of bulrushes beside the shore.

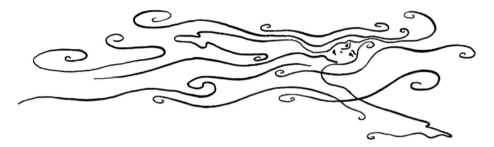

"That's the way to the Lost Lagoon!" shouted Jeremy Mouse, pointing.

"Where?" asked Pine Cone and Pepper Pot.

Jeremy Mouse pointed again—but all they could see were bulrushes.

"How do you know?" asked Greenleaf.

"The Lady under the Water," said Jeremy Mouse. "She told me."

Everyone looked into the river, but there was no one there.

"That must have been the Spirit of Running River," said Tiptoes happily. "Why didn't I think of asking her? Good for you, Jeremy Mouse!" and she patted him on the back.

Greenleaf guided the boat towards the shore and wound carefully in and out of the bulrushes. Whenever they found their way blocked they soon saw another channel that led further inland. Bit by bit they went forward, until at last they spied a dense clump of oak trees. They were huge and old and mysterious. The channel meandered this way and that, but always the oak grove drew closer. The air became still and hot, and over their heads dozens of dragonflies flitted lightly back and forth, their silvery wings glistening with many colors.

At last they reached the grove and the channel led them in amongst the great oaks. There they were; they had found the Lost Lagoon, hidden beneath the trees!

"Oh, goody," exclaimed Jeremy Mouse. "Now we can eat!"

# 27

# *The Lost Lagoon*

Greenleaf sailed his boat into the Lost Lagoon. The whole lagoon lay underneath the huge oak trees, its waters resting quietly in the shade. Now and then a splash broke the silence, or they heard a squirrel scampering high overhead in the canopy. Massive trunks rose majestically out of the still water, their branches arching overhead and making a roof like a cathedral.

"It's like a church," whispered Pine Cone, afraid to speak loudly.

"Yes, it is," agreed Tiptoes. "It's magical! See how everything is mirrored in the water."

"How did it get here?" asked Jeremy Mouse.

"Running River flowed here a long time ago," answered Greenleaf. "But she wandered away and left a hollow in the ground. The trees came and covered the whole hollow over. Now the river only returns when her floods are extra high. Then, for a short while, the trees stand deep in water."

The air was cool and soft inside the grove. Here and there rays of sunlight broke through the leaves high above them. The rays played amongst the branches or fell into the water with a splash of light.

In and out between the trees the leaf boat wandered, looking for a place to land. At last they found a branch sloping gently out of the water. Greenleaf brought his boat alongside the branch and hopped lightly out. He held the prow as Jeremy Mouse and the gnomes clambered out. Tiptoes followed, carrying the brightly colored cloth that held the muffins. She opened the cloth, spread it out on the branch, and they sat down to eat.

"I'm starving!" said Jeremy Mouse, looking at the muffins with hungry eyes.

"First we say grace," said Tiptoes firmly, and they all took hands:

> *"Bless these muffins*
> *So yummy and nice—*
> *I know they'll be loved*
> *By fairies and mice ...*
> *Especially mice!"*

"Amen," said Pine Cone and Pepper Pot, their pointy caps sending off little sparks.

"Me too!" said Jeremy Mouse. "Can I have the Mouse Tail muffin first?"

Tiptoes nodded and laughed. "Yes," she said. "I made it just for you."

# 28

## *The Sobbing One*

Jeremy Mouse was happy. He'd eaten four muffins altogether and his belly was full. Tiptoes and Greenleaf had shared a blueberry muffin, and Pine Cone and Pepper Pot had gone halves with a biscuit. Jeremy Mouse was right; fairies didn't eat much. Now they were resting and enjoying the lagoon. The water was as smooth as glass and everything was perfectly mirrored in its surface. It created a beautiful space filled with tree trunks and branches, sunlight and water.

Jeremy was beginning to doze off—but something kept bothering him. Far away he heard a dripping sound ... drip-drip, drip-drip ... followed by sobbing. He perked up his ears and listened ... but all he heard was the quiet buzzing of insects.

He was just about to snooze again, when there it was ... drip-drip, drip-drip, sob-sob-sobbing.

"Tiptoes," said Jeremy Mouse, "do you hear a dripping sound? I also hear sobbing."

"I thought I heard something," answered Tiptoes, "but I wasn't sure."

"Me too," said Greenleaf. "You'd better go see what it is, Tiptoes. We'll follow in the boat."

Tiptoes opened her wings and flitted into the air. In and out between the trees she flew, seeking and searching. It was hard to tell where the sound was coming from and she often had to stop and listen. At last she spotted tiny drops of water falling in pairs from the end of a branch. As they fell into the lagoon two delicate circles spread out and quickly disappeared.

Tiptoes flew closer and found a slug sitting on the branch. He was sobbing and sobbing, and the tears from his eyestalks were falling, drip-drip, into the water.

"Oh, Slug," said Tiptoes, concerned, "what's the matter? Why are you crying?"

The slug slowly turned his head and looked at Tiptoes.

"Oh, you'll never understand," he sobbed. "We slugs have such sorrows heaped upon us," and he let out a huge sigh.

"Why's that?" asked Tiptoes. "What wrong?"

"What's wrong!" cried the slug in surprise. "Look at me! Can't you see?"

Tiptoes looked at the slug. He seemed perfectly fine to her.

"I don't see anything wrong," said Tiptoes, scratching her head. "You look fine to me."

"No! No! No!" groaned the slug. "Look again! It's not what you see. It's what you *don't* see!"

Tiptoes was puzzled and looked carefully at the slug again.

"I don't see anything," she said at last, shrugging her shoulders. "I mean, I can't see the something that I'm supposed to be not seeing."

"Of course you can't see anything," said the slug, getting exasperated. "That's because it's *not there!* It's *missing!*"

Tiptoes scratched her head again. Now she was really puzzled. Slugs were much more complicated than she'd thought.

"You can't see anything because it's *gone!*" wailed the slug, huge tears flowing from his eyes and dripping into the water. "Gone! Gone! Gone! I've been searching everywhere my whole life!"

"But what's gone?" asked Tiptoes. "Tell me what's missing!"

"My house!" bawled the slug, swaying his head from side to side in the air. "Can't you see? My house is missing! Oh, it's such a tragedy … such a tragedy!"

"I've often wondered why slugs don't have shells," said Tiptoes. " But I thought you were just made that way."

"Oh, no!" moaned the slug. "Not at all! We all had shells, beautiful house-shells, every one of us."

"But how did you lose them?" asked Tiptoes.

"I'll tell you," sobbed the slug mournfully. "I'll tell you the whole sorry tale. It's the saddest tale in the whole wide world."

71

# 29

## *The Saddest Slug Tale in the Whole Wide World*

"Once upon a time, a very long time ago, snails were huge, as big as elephants, even bigger—some were as big as ships. They sailed around on their silvery roads and munched on trees. Sometimes hundreds of them gathered together around a stony mountain called Castle Hill and shot darts at each other. They had a special dart sack inside them that held the darts. They'd sail past each other, just like ships in the olden days, and shoot the darts from their sides like cannons. If a dart hit a snail's shell it would bounce off harmlessly. But when a snail's foot was hit, he'd say things like, 'Ouch!' or 'Eeek!' and curl up inside his house until the battle was over and it was safe to come out. The last snail standing was the winner. He climbed to the top of Castle Hill, and shouted: 'I'm the king of the Castle and you're the dirty rascals!' Then all the snails would come out and start the battle again, for it was really just a game.

And to this day children play games like King of the Castle—though they don't know why they say 'I'm the king of the castle' when they are on top of the hill. And snails still shoot darts at each other—but only if they are in love and want to get the other snail's attention."

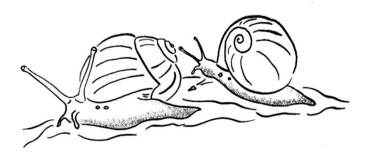

Tiptoes looked at the slug in astonishment. "Snails shooting darts! That can't be true!" she said. "I've never heard such a thing!"

"It's true," said the slug. "Look it up and see for yourself."

"Anyways," he continued, "there was one snail who didn't like battles, even if they were just a game. 'Battles are such silly things,' he said to himself. 'Charging around and shooting darts and saying 'Eeek' and 'Ouch' is not for me. I have better things to do.'

The truth was, however, that this snail was very proud of his shell and didn't want it damaged. And he did have a lovely shell. It wound upwards in a smooth spiral of creamy brown stripes like a candy cane.

One day, as the snail was wandering around, he came upon a lady snail. She was gorgeously good-looking, with a long, extra-slimy foot and a beautiful shell covered with pretty spots.

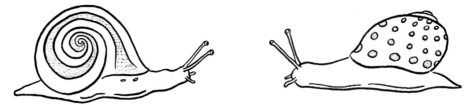

"Oh, what a beautiful shell you have," exclaimed the he-snail.

The lady snail was flattered and dipped her eyestalks demurely to the ground.

"Oh, no," she replied politely, "you have a much more handsome shell than I. I love your creamy brown stripes and smooth spiral. Your shell is much more magnificent than mine!"

"Thank you," said the he-snail courteously, "but really, your shell is so much finer than mine! I would much rather have your sumptuous spots than my silky stripes."

Back and forth the two snails complimented each other, not wanting to be outdone by the other, and always saying (even though it wasn't really true) that they would much rather have the other snail's shell for a house, until, in the end, there was nothing left for the he-snail to do but gallantly offer to swap shells. And the lady snail had made such a fuss about the he-snail's shell that there was nothing else to do but accept.

And so they crawled out of their shells (blushing just a little bit to be seen without their houses on) and slowly slid towards their new homes. But right at that moment a Storm Dragon came raging over Castle Hill, shaking trees and sending leaves flying. The Storm Dragon's wings whipped dust and sand into the air and the snails had to pull their eyes inside their heads. Then, as quickly as he had come, the Storm Dragon was gone. The snails opened their eyes, and their houses, their beautiful houses, were gone! Gone! Gone! Gone! Their wonderful shells had vanished!"

"Oh! Oh! Oh!" wailed the slug. "The wind had whisked their houses away! And even though they searched their whole lives they never found them. Then their children searched, and their children's children searched, and still to this day we search, always seeking, always hoping to find our beautiful shells."

Tiptoes looked at the slug and shook her head.

"I never knew your true story," she said. "What a sad tale!"

"Oh, yes! Yes!" agreed the slug sorrowfully. "We have the sorriest tale in the whole world. Whenever you see us slugs sailing along, you can be sure we are looking for our lost shells," and he slowly turned and sailed away on his silvery road.

# 30

# *A Spider from on high*

Greenleaf watched as Tiptoes flew away, her golden wings sparkling as she wove in and out of the tree trunks. Then they all clambered into the leaf boat and set off. At first Greenleaf followed Tiptoes as she flitted here and there, but she was soon out of sight. They stopped every now and then to listen for the sobbing, but after a while there was nothing to be heard.

"Tiptoes must have found whoever was crying," said Greenleaf. "I don't hear the sobbing anymore."

"Me neither," agreed Pine Cone, "but let's keep looking."

They came upon a turtle lying on a log.

"Have you seen Tiptoes Lightly?" asked Pepper Pot.

"I did," answered the turtle, "but by the time I said 'hello' she was already gone. She flies fast!"

They searched some more, checking nooks and crannies along the shore and exploring between the trees, but Tiptoes was not to be found.

"We'll have to wait till she comes back and finds us," said Greenleaf. "What else can we do?"

So they sat in the boat and waited. A pair of magpies chased each other in the treetops and a woodpecker flew from tree to tree with strong, powerful strokes. A tiny wren flitted past. He circled around and landed on a nearby twig. He looked at them with dark, shiny eyes. Then he flicked his short sticking-up tail and flew away.

Jeremy Mouse gazed at the canopy arching above them. The leaf boat lay so still that he felt as if he was floating on air. He watched a spider descending on a long, thin thread from high above the boat. Now and then the thread caught the sunlight and glinted brightly before it vanished again. Down and down and down the spider came, hanging in the air as lightly as a feather until he was just above their heads. Pepper Pot looked up and saw the spider too.

"It's Spin-a-lot!" he exclaimed. "What are you doing here?"

"Visiting the Lost Lagoon," said Spin-a-lot. "I heard from the frogs that the flying was extra good here—so I came."

"How do you do that?" Jeremy Mouse blurted out in amazement.

"Do what?" asked Spin-a-lot, looking puzzled.

"Make such a long, long thread! You must have a huge spool hidden inside of you!"

"Yes! Yes!" nodded Pine Cone. "I've often wondered about that too! A huge spool of thread! That's a good idea!"

Greenleaf and Pepper Pot bobbed their heads in agreement.

Spin-a-lot scratched his chin with one of his eight spindly legs. "I'm not sure how I do it," he replied. "I just do. Maybe there is a huge spool of thread inside of me! But what are you folks doing here?"

"We've lost Tiptoes Lightly," said Jeremy Mouse.

"Lost Tiptoes Lightly!" exclaimed Spin-a-lot. "What happened? Where did she go?"

"We don't know," answered Greenleaf. "We heard someone sobbing and she went to find out who it was. Now we can't find her. We're waiting."

"Oh! I love waiting!" declared Spin-a-lot. "It's so much fun! Sometimes it's so much fun I just can't wait to wait! Can I wait with you? *Please?*"

"Of course you can wait with us," said Greenleaf, "... if you really want to."

76

"Oh, thank you! Thank you!" gushed Spin-a-lot, rubbing his legs together and settling down.

Jeremy Mouse, Greenleaf the Sailor, Pine Cone and Pepper Pot looked at Spin-a-lot the Spider, and Spin-a-lot the Spider looked at Pepper Pot, Pine Cone, Greenleaf the Sailor and Jeremy Mouse.

Five minutes passed and they were still looking at each other.

Then another five minutes …

And another five minutes …

"This is boring," said Jeremy Mouse, getting restless.

"I can wait a long time," offered Spin-a-lot cheerfully. "I adore waiting! It's the best thing in the whole world! Sometimes, after I've spun a web, I get to wait for days and days for a fly to come along. I love it!"

Jeremy Mouse looked at Spin-a-lot some more. He didn't like waiting. It made him fidgety.

"Why don't you tell us a tale, Spin-a-lot," he said at last.

"A spider story!" cried Greenleaf, suddenly looking interested and sitting upright in the boat. "That's a good idea! Tell us a spider tale."

"Yes, yes," agreed the gnomes. They had been getting restless too.

Spin-a-lot the Spider scratched his head and thought hard. Spiders have lots of stories and love to spin tales.

"I know," he said at last. "I'll tell you a Long Legs story. This one's called, 'Long Legs the Spider and how he saved the world.'"

# 31

## *Long Legs the Spider*
## *and*
## *how he saved the World*

"A long time ago there lived a spider. He had a round body like a button, and eight long, spindly legs. He also had eight skinny knees, eight slim ankles, eight bony feet and no toes at all. His name was Long Legs—which was a very common name amongst spiders of his sort. So common, in fact, that if you wave to a crowd of his kind, and shout: 'Yoo-hoo! Long Legs!' all of them will turn around and look at you.

One day, as Long Legs was spinning his web, two birds landed in a bush close by. One bird said to the other: 'Cousin Sparrow, we are in trouble. The mighty eagle, King Prez, King of Birds, has lost a feather, and we are the ones to find it. If we don't, King Prez says the sky will fall and squash us into pancakes.'

'That sounds like Chicken Little,' replied Cousin Sparrow. 'He thought the sky was falling too, but he was just being a silly goose.'

'That's true, Cousin Sparrow, but this time it's for real—King Prez says so—and if we don't find that feather, it's pancakes for all of us!'

Long Legs ran, linkety-lank, to his brothers and sisters. 'King Prez has lost a feather!' he cried. 'If we don't find it the sky will squish us into pancakes!'

'Which feather did he lose?' asked his littlest sister.

'The feather from his cap, for sure,' said his second eldest brother. 'It's the biggest feather; it holds the universe up!'

'Oh, no!' moaned all the spiders. 'Not the feather from King Prez's cap!' and they began to wail as if the world was going to end.

'Stop wailing and collect your wits,' shouted Long Legs. 'Run to the four corners of the earth. Search under every stone. Spin webs and catch flies … I mean, spin webs and catch spies, maybe they know something!'

So all the long-legged spiders ran, linkety-lank, around the world, spinning webs and catching spies and looking under stones. But the feather was not to be found.

Just then a tortoise came lumbering by.

'What's all the fuss about?' he asked. 'You'd think the world was ending!'

'It is! It is!' Long Legs cried. 'The feather from King Prez's cap is not to be found! We'll be squished into pancakes!'

'Nonsense!' said the tortoise. 'I'm the one that holds the sky up with my strong shell. Just tell King Prez that you found the feather and put it back in his cap. He'll never notice it's not true.'

So all the spiders ran linkety-lank to King Prez, and said: 'O, King Prez, we found the feather from your cap and put it back—you look so high and mighty!'

'Thank goodness,' sighed King Prez, much relieved. 'Now the sky will not fall and no one will be flattened into pancakes.'

'Hurrah!' cried all the spiders.

'Hurray!' cried all the birds.

'I'm hungry,' declared King Prez. 'Where are my cooks?'

All the cooks came crawling out of the royal kitchen on their humble hands and knees.

'What's for breakfast?' demanded the King.

'Pancakes, your majesty,' they replied, bowing up and down and scraping the floor.

'Pancakes!' exclaimed the spiders in dismay. And in a flash they all ran away as linkety-lank fast as their skinny legs could carry them!"

"That's a good spider's tale," said Greenleaf. "My mother used to tell me about Long Legs when I was little too."

"Us too," chimed in the gnomes.

Just then Tiptoes came flying through the air and landed in the boat.

"I met a slug and he told me the strangest tale," she said breathlessly. "I flew back as fast as I could—I can't wait to tell it to you."

"We've had a story as well," said Jeremy Mouse, pointing to Spin-a-lot. "Let's swap tales."

And so they did.

# 32

# *A Nest for the Night*

They watched as Spin-a-lot the Spider climbed back up his slim rope. Up, and up, and up he climbed until they couldn't see him anymore.

"Goodbye, Spin-a-lot," called Jeremy Mouse.

"Goodbye," called the fairies. "Goodbye."

For the rest of the afternoon they explored the Lost Lagoon. They found frogs aplenty and saw dozens of bird's nests in the branches. Tiptoes decided to search along the skirts of the grove. She liked finding plants and asking them their names or hearing their tales. She found a tumble weed that told her the storm had tumbled it all the way from the top of the bluffs. She discovered a small plant with a yellow flower called Blow Wives, and another that looked like a daisy who called herself Tidy Tips. Then she met a Hogwallow Starfish, some Butter and Eggs, a bunch of Parrot Feathers, and a crowd of lovely Red Maids.

Jeremy Mouse came over and joined her. He searched around and found a small plant with very thin leaves that he'd never seen before.

"What are you called?" he asked.

"My name's Tiny Mouse Tail," it answered.

"Tiny Mouse Tail!" exclaimed Jeremy Mouse, and he looked carefully at the leaves. "That's right," he agreed. "You do have tiny mouse tails— except yours are green."

Pine Cone and Pepper Pot joined in the hunt too. Pepper Pot found a plant called Sneezeweed—though it hadn't flowered yet. If he'd found it in fall when it flowered then he definitely would have sneezed!

Pine Cone came across a strange plant growing low to the ground. It was small, with leaves like fingers held in a cup. In the middle of the cup was a flower that looked like a blob of sheep's wool. He called everybody over to see.

"That's a funny looking flower you have," said Pine Cone, bending over the plant. "All woolly like a sheep."

"Or some kind of strange beard," added Pepper Pot.

The gnomes thought that this was the funniest plant they'd seen in a long time.

"What's your name, little woolly one?" they asked.

The plant was shy and its voice so soft that they all had to put their ears close to the ground to hear what it had to say.

"I'm called Dwarf Woolly-Heads," it whispered, a small smile hidden in its voice. "Have you seen any others hereabouts?" it added. "Apart from you two gnomes, that is?"

The look on the gnome's faces was so funny that Jeremy Mouse laughed until his tail was sore.

Late in the afternoon they ate supper on the edge of the grove. The fairies had one muffin apiece, while Jeremy Mouse ate all the rest. Then they went hunting for nuts and seeds because Jeremy Mouse was still hungry.

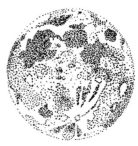

Slowly the sun sank in the sky and the shadows grew long. Flights of duck and Canada geese glided down to spend the night on Running River. They climbed back into the boat and sailed over the quiet waters of the Lost Lagoon. Just then the frogs began their evening chorus:

> *"Under ancient oaken trees these waters ...*
> *Waxing full in flood from river running ...*
> *Know the secret moon-tide song of love that ...*
> *We the frogs this silver night are singing ..."*

The oak trees were glowing warmly in the last rays of the sun as they climbed into an old woodpecker's nest that Greenleaf had found. The nest was high up the tree trunk, but worth the climb. It was clean and dry, and filled with downy feathers, soft moss and grass.

Jeremy Mouse lay looking out of the doorway. Lost Lagoon was wrapped in darkness, while here and there a star twinkled through the leaves. He was still listening to the frogs singing when he finally closed his eyes and went to sleep.

> *"Hear the voice of us, O you the silver ...*
> *One who rides amongst the stars this evening ...*
> *Sending down your rays of sun transforméd ...*
> *Into life that rises in us dreaming ..."*

Then silently, majestically, the full round moon rose into the night sky over the Snowy Mountains.

# 33

## *Farmer John reads to the Children*

Farmer John trudged towards the house from his fields. It was already getting dark and the full moon was rising when he opened the kitchen door.

"Woof! Woof!" barked Lucy gently. That was his way of saying hello. He wagged his tail furiously and panted with a huge grin on his face.

June Berry came running down the stairs with Tom hard at her heels. They were already in their pajamas.

"Dad! Did you see the moon? It's huge!" June Berry said. "We saw it out the window."

"I did see the moon," said Farmer John. "It's full tonight."

"Where did you go?" asked Tom.

"I took Chiron to the upper meadow. Now that the rains are gone it's dry enough for him to spend the night there. He much prefers to be outside."

"Let's read 'The Adam Tales'," said June Berry, grabbing her dad's hand and pulling.

"Wait a minute, young filly!" laughed Farmer John. "Let me get my coat off and wash my hands. We'll read upstairs tonight."

Tom and June charged for the stairs.

"The book! The book!" called Farmer John after them.

The children stopped in mid flight—they'd forgotten the book in the living room. In an instant they were charging the other way.

Farmer John chuckled and took off his coat. When he got upstairs the children were waiting for him. They were sitting on June Berry's bed. Soon they were cuddled up and ready to start.

"Now, where were we?" asked Farmer John, opening the book and turning the pages. "Oh, yes! Here it is: *Why the Pot was moved the third Time.*"

# 34

## Why the Pot was moved the third Time

Once upon a time a pot sat on the shores of an ancient river. Some animals saw it and thought it a strange object indeed—for this was in the days before the first human being walked upon the earth.

"That is a strange thing," said the elephant. "I have never seen such a shape. It must be a new kind of animal."

"But where are its legs?" asked the springbok. "An animal *must* have legs!"

"No, it mustn't!" hissed the snake, annoyed at such a thought.

"And where's its tail?" barked the baboon, holding his long tail high in the air and swishing it back and forth. "A proper animal must have a tail!"

"That's not true!" croaked the bullfrog. "Not all animals have tails! Look at me!"

"You once had a tail when you were small," said the baboon, "but it fell off and became a fish."

The bullfrog rolled his eyes at such silliness and didn't bother to reply. Everyone knew that a tadpole's tail was touched by the tadpole fairy and turned into all the hops a frog ever took.

85

"And this thing does not have horns," said the kudu, who was very proud of his long, twisty horns.

"Nor gills," shouted the fish. He had to shout because he couldn't leave the river to get close to where everyone was standing.

"Nor tusks and sticking-out teeth," snuffled the ugly warthog.

"Nor proper spots," purred the leopard.

"Nor a proper squirm," murmured the worm, sticking his head out of the ground.

"Perhaps it's an egg," said the ostrich. "I'll sit on it and see if it hatches," and she sat on top of the pot and fluffed up her feathers.

"No! No!" cried all the animals. "Don't sit on it! What if it hatches? That could be dangerous!"

But too late! The ostrich had already gone all broody, with a faraway look in her eyes. The animals knew there was no use talking to her anymore and that she just wouldn't listen.

Now I have to tell you that in those long-ago times not all animals looked the same as they do now. Back then, ostriches were covered from head to toe with large, fluffy feathers. When the ostrich sat on the pot and pulled in her long neck she looked just like a big ball of feathers.

"What shall we do? What shall we do?" trumpeted the elephant in despair. "We can't let her hatch the egg!"

"Push her off!" shouted the kudu. "Quickly!"

So they pushed and pushed the ostrich … but she wouldn't budge an inch.

"I know," said the baboon, "let's pull her off. I'll grab her neck and two of my brothers can grab her legs."

So the three baboons grabbed the ostrich and pulled, and pulled, and pulled. But the ostrich still didn't move an inch.

"Pull harder!" cried the tortoise.

"Yes! Yes!" agreed all the other animals. "Pull harder!"

So the baboons pulled even harder. They pulled, and pulled, and pulled. Suddenly all three fell backwards in a flurry of feathers. When the feathers had settled to the ground the ostrich was still sitting on the pot—but her long neck and legs had been stripped bare.

"Squawk!" screeched the ostrich, waking up from her broodiness and feeling very naked. Up she jumped and took off faster than a bird had ever run before!

"Now look at what you've done!" grunted the warthog.

"We didn't have any choice!" howled the baboons.

"That's right," agreed the elephant. "They didn't have any choice. But I am going to get rid of this thing.

It is too dangerous to leave lying around." He picked up the pot with his trunk and threw it over his head with all his might.

"There," he said, very satisfied with himself, "now it's gone, and we'll never be bothered by it again."

But the pot just sailed through the air, over the bushes, over the trees, and landed with a splash in the river. Up and down it bobbed, and the river carried it away and left it lying on the shores of an island.

And that's what happened to the pot the third time—and also why ostriches are the fastest runners of all the birds on the earth, don't have any feathers on their necks and legs, and look a little naked and silly. If you don't believe me you can go to Africa and ask an ostrich yourself; she will tell you the very same story.

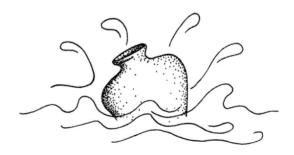

# 35

# *Pine Cone and Pepper Pot wake up*

Pine Cone and Pepper Pot were fast asleep in the woodpecker's nest. Slowly the moon swung into the starry sky until her silvery light shimmered through the doorway.

"Wake! Awake!" the moon whispered to the gnomes. "It's time! It's time!"

Pine Cone stirred and tossed from side to side. He sat up, opened his eyes, and looked around. Pepper Pot was snoring.

"Wake up, Pepper Pot!" he called softly. "It's time!"

But Pepper Pot only grunted and turned over.

Pine Cone stuck out his foot and gave Pepper Pot a shove. It can be hard to wake Pepper Pot up when he's deep asleep.

"Wake up, Pepper Pot!" he called again.

Pepper Pot mumbled in his sleep and began to snore even louder. Pine Cone poked him with his foot again—and not so gently this time.

"What? Who?" shouted Pepper Pot, sitting up with a start and looking around wildly. "Who's punching me?"

"It's just me," said Pine Cone, "and I wasn't punching you. You're impossible to wake up! But look! The moon's up. She's calling us! It's time!"

The gnomes unwrapped their beards from around their heads and put on their red hats. Instantly their pointy tips began to sparkle.

Pine Cone tapped Greenleaf on the shoulder and woke him too.

"It's time, Greenleaf," he said. "You have to bring us to the shore."

Greenleaf got up and they climbed down the tree. His leaf boat had drifted away out of sight into the lagoon. He called it to him in a whisper.

> *"Little Leaf*
> *So green and bright—*
> *Come out of hiding*
> *Into sight!"*

And the little boat came drifting over the silvery waters of the Lost Lagoon.

They climbed in and Greenleaf quietly called: "Sail, little boat! Sail!" and off the little boat sailed until they reached the shore.

"Thank you, Greenleaf," said the gnomes, stepping ashore. "We'll see you tomorrow."

They watched as Greenleaf sailed away, but wondered why he didn't return to the woodpecker's nest.

From their pockets they took out the small silvery buckets and feathers they'd brought and into the moonlight the gnomes marched. All along the edge of the oak grove they went a-hunting for the moonlight that's caught in spider webs and dew drops. Then, using the silver feathers, they brushed the moonlight into their buckets. They sang quietly as they worked:

> *"Silver light, lovely sight,*
> *Fill our buckets full and bright."*

They wandered across the marshes and over to Running River. There they gathered the silver glistening on the water and caught the sparkles from the backs of minnows. Everywhere they went they swept and dusted the silvery moonlight into their buckets until they were full.

90

Off to the bluffs they strode and into a crack in the cliff that led to winding stairs. Down, down the stairs they marched, round and round, deeper and deeper into the earth. At last they reached the bottom and wandered along a tunnel that twisted and turned until they came to an underground cave. It was a silver cave, with the purest silver running through the rocks in rivers.

On the night of the full moon all the silver in the earth begins to flow. It makes the most wonderful streams of glimmering light. Pine Cone and Pepper Pot emptied their buckets into the largest river and watched as the precious metal flowed away. For all their hard work the gnomes had only the tiniest amount of silver. But everywhere on the earth, wherever the full moon shone brightly, thousands of gnomes were gathering silver too and bringing it into the rocks below. That's how the silver that men love so much comes to be inside the earth—though many men have forgotten it and don't give proper thanks to the gnomes when they take it.

Pine Cone and Pepper Pot had worked so hard and for so long that they stayed in the silver cave. They climbed into a comfy nook in the rock, wound their long beards round their tired heads, and fell fast asleep.

# 36

## *Tom goes out in the Moonlight*

Tom Nutcracker lay in bed. He couldn't sleep. The full moon shone brightly through his window and made him restless. Now and then he heard Chiron whinnying far over the fields in the upper meadow.

Tom climbed out of bed, pulled on his clothes, and snuck out of the house. He walked across the fields towards the upper meadow. The moon was so bright he could see the dew on the grass and Running River glistening in the distance. Patches of mist floated on the river, or reached ghostly fingers inland onto the low-lying fields.

Chiron whinnied and galloped over when Tom reached the meadow. He nuzzled Tom's face and checked his hands for treats. Tom opened the gate and let himself in. He stood next to Chiron for a moment, making up his mind. Then he grabbed Chiron's mane and swung himself up. He dug in his heels and over the meadow they galloped towards the further gate.

After this gate there were no more fences, or at least not for a long while. A horse track cut through scrubland and into the forest. Then it turned and followed Running River upstream towards the Snowy Mountains.

Tom didn't stop at all, but neither did he rush. He kept Chiron at a steady canter until he reached Running River. He rode upstream until he came to the bluffs. At the top of the bluff he stopped next to the tree overhanging the cliff so dangerously. He stayed on Chiron. He felt safe there and Chiron's body kept him warm.

Tom looked over the landscape. In the distance the snow on the mountains glistened silvery-gray. Here and there a cloud clung to a mountain peak, but otherwise the night was clear and filled with stars.

Tom gazed upriver. The horse path got narrower after the bluffs and less certain. He saw the huge grove of oak trees that he'd always wanted to visit. They looked dark and mysterious and full of secrets. Tom had never dared to go so far from home by himself, but tonight seemed different. He felt completely unafraid and safe. So down the far side of the bluffs he trotted, heading for the Lost Lagoon.

# 37

## *Tom goes to the Lost Lagoon*

Tom could see the grove, but didn't know how to get there. The ground was soft and Chiron kept stumbling into flood water. At last he found a thin ribbon of high ground that made its way towards the grove. Tom followed it and rode slowly forward. As he came closer, the trees loomed large and mysterious. Everything was still and quiet. The air, which had been so warm during the day, was damp and chilly. Tom felt lucky to have Chiron beneath him.

When they reached the grove he saw that he couldn't ride around it. The land all about was swamped. He rode under the branches of the trees, but he'd hardly reached the trunk of the first massive oak when Chiron's feet splashed into water. Chiron stopped. Tom urged him on. Chiron reluctantly stepped forward and immediately the water became deeper. Chiron backed out and stood still. He wasn't going to go forward.

Tom let his eyes get used to the darkness. Gradually the space beneath the trees took shape. Instead of solid land, Tom saw a glistening sheet of still water. He could tell the lagoon was deep because the tree trunks were hidden and only their branches reached out of the water.

Moonlight filtered through the leaves high above Tom's head. The grove was calm and the water like a sheet of finest glass — except for a tiny ripple moving towards him from out in the lagoon. At first Tom thought it was a fish swimming just below the surface, its fin marking its path through the water. But, as it came closer, he saw that it was a leaf. Tom couldn't work out why the leaf was moving all by itself, but it was. Tom was so curious that he slid off Chiron's back and hunkered down at the water's edge. He waited, looking intently.

As the leaf drew near he saw that it was a leaf boat, strangely and beautifully shaped—like a Viking ship. In the boat stood a small man, no bigger than his little finger, even smaller! Tom froze. He couldn't believe what he was seeing. For a moment he wondered if he'd fallen asleep and was dreaming. The leaf boat stopped in front of him.

"Hello, Tom," the little man said in a clear voice.

Tom didn't know what to say. He was dumbstruck.

"Tiptoes Lightly told me about you," the little man added. "That's how I know your name. And that's Chiron the Pony, isn't it?"

Tom nodded. At last he understood that this wasn't a human being.

"Are you a dwarf?" he asked.

"No," said the little man, bright sparks flickering in his eyes. "I'm an elf. I live beside Running River not far from your house."

"Where?" asked Tom.

"Beside the big willow in your dad's forest," the man replied.

Tom nodded understandingly. He knew this tree well.

"What's your name?" he asked.

"They call me Greenleaf the Sailor around here. Would you like to come sailing with me?"

Tom chucked. "Your boat is much too small."

"No, it's not," said Greenleaf, a mischievous smile on his lips. "Get in."

"How can I get in?" asked Tom. "I'm far too big."

"Your body is too big," said Greenleaf. "But you're not. Get in!"

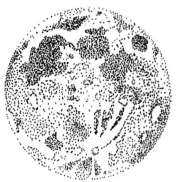

Tom understood. He focused intently on the boat and stepped inside.

"That's better," said Greenleaf, patting him on the back. "Let's be off."

Greenleaf called out: *"Sail, little boat! Sail!"* and off the boat glided over the lagoon.

Tom's eyes seemed so much sharper. His ears heard small, faraway sounds, and he could even smell how smooth the water was. In the center of the lagoon the trees opened and let in a large beam of moonlight. Greenleaf sailed into the light. Tom looked up and saw the moon above him. He felt a strange pulling sensation, as if he was being drawn out of himself. He'd felt this before at full moon, but now it was much stronger.

Then Greenleaf cried: *"Up, little boat! Up!"* and the leaf boat lifted into the air and followed the moonbeam out of the Lost Lagoon.

# 38

## *Greenleaf and Tom sail to the Moon*

Greenleaf followed the moonbeam all the way to the moon. Tom saw a silver fence stretching far into the distance. On one side were planets and stars, and on the other side sat Mother Earth with a seed in her cupped hands. In the middle of the fence was a gate. From one direction young children were pouring in, and from the other old people were passing out. Where they met they stopped and talked, passing news to each other of what lay ahead on their journey.

"What's that gate?" asked Tom, pointing. He felt a great longing to go through the gate towards the stars.

"The Moon Gate," Greenleaf replied.

"Are we going through?" Tom asked.

Greenleaf smiled. "You came through that gate just a short time ago, Tom. That's why you could get into my boat so easily. When you're an old, old man you'll go through that gate again. But first you have tasks to do and adventures to take."

Tom watched the comings and goings for a long time. Now and then an angel passed through the Moon Gate too. If they were going towards the earth they changed shape and became small and human, and if they were leaving the earth they suddenly grew wings filled with the most beautiful eyes and flew away to the stars. At last Greenleaf turned his boat and followed the moonbeam back to the Lost Lagoon.

At the shore Chiron was waiting patiently. Tom jumped onto his back and turned towards home. Although it seemed like a long time had passed, Tom saw that the moon was not much higher in the sky. Still, he felt he should hurry. As soon as it was safe he set Chiron at a gallop. Over the bluff they ran, down along the river, through the forest and over the scrublands.

When they arrived at the upper meadow he saw how sweaty Chiron had become and knew he could not leave him outside to catch a chill. He brought Chiron to the barn, rubbed him down and put his horse blanket on. Tom was worried. If he didn't take Chiron back to the meadow before his father got up in the morning there would be questions to answer.

So Tom did second best. He led Chiron back to the meadow but left his horse blanket on. That way he stayed warm and Tom had a better chance of getting to Chiron before his dad did—or so he hoped.

# 39

## *Tiptoes wakes in the Night*

Tiptoes woke in the night. She stood in the doorway of the woodpecker's nest high above the lagoon. The full moon had risen and everything was glowing with silvery light: the leaves were silver, the tree trunks were silver, and the water far below glistened with silver.

Out into the air Tiptoes leapt. Down, down she dove, her arms spread out like wings. Then she opened her real wings and skimmed along the water like a swallow. Her sky-blue dress glimmered with silver, her hair shone with silver, even her golden wings shimmered with the silvery light of the moon.

Then up, up, up she soared, through the roof of the oak grove and high into the sky. Far below she saw the silvery path of Running River glinting in the moonlight as it flowed to the sea. Marshes and wetlands, spread out on either side, were frosted with silver, and in the East, moonlight sparkled on the silvery-white peaks of the Snowy Mountains. She turned to the West and saw on the distant ocean a moon-path riding on the waves.

Tiptoes looked at the moonlight with her fairy eyes. Hosts of moon beings were streaming down to earth and disappearing into the plants and stones. She also saw the moonlight flowing back to the moon again, carrying earth secrets into the sky. It was like a great, delicate tide soaring upwards in waves.

For a long time Tiptoes watched the earth and moon speaking to each other. Then, at midnight, a hush fell across the land, and the Moon Princess came gliding towards her on a moonbeam. She was beautiful and royal, with a majestic, silvery dress, long silvery hair and silver eyes. Around her neck hung a string of twenty-eight silver pearls.

"Good evening, little fairy," said the Moon Princess. "I see that you are a child of the sun and wind."

"Yes, I am," answered Tiptoes, curtsying low. She was astonished that the Moon Princess had spoken to her.

"Then why are you up so late in the night?"

"Because I love the moonlight. It feels cool on my wings and has so many secrets within it."

The Moon Princess smiled at Tiptoes. She liked her reply. She reached into her pocket and took out a delicate silver chain. Hanging from the chain was a small, round disk, finely set about with tiny pearls. The Moon Princess reached out to Tiptoes and put it around her neck. It fit perfectly.

Tiptoes bowed deeply at being given such a gift. She didn't know what to say. She took the small disk in her hand and looked at it. It seemed like a silver mirror, but when she gazed into it she didn't see her reflection. She saw instead the golden sun shining in the sky! From the sun were seven swans flying, a white cloth held in their beaks. On the cloth sat a child, and the child held the earth in his hands.

"Thank you, Moon Princess," said Tiptoes, bowing deeply again. "I shall treasure this gift always."

"You are most welcome, child of sun and wind. Now isn't it time for little fairies to be in bed?"

Tiptoes smiled and nodded her head. She knew that this was the Moon Princess's way of telling her it was time to go.

So down, down Tiptoes glided, her hair streaming out behind her in the silvery air. Round and round she flew, lower and lower … into the oak grove that covered the Lost Lagoon … in amongst the tree trunks and branches, and into the woodpecker's nest. Then she folded her wings, lay quietly down, and fell fast asleep.

# 40

## *Jeremy Mouse sleeps like a Log*

Jeremy Mouse didn't wake up in the night. He slept like a log. In the morning the sun peeked into the woodpecker's nest.

"Good morning, Jeremy Mouse," called the sun. "Time to wake up, you sleepyhead!"

Jeremy Mouse yawned and stretched, and opened his eyes. Tiptoes and Greenleaf were sitting in the doorway. They were talking quietly about all the things they'd seen and heard in the night.

"Good morning, Jeremy Mouse," said Tiptoes, turning around.

"Good morning, sleepyhead," laughed Greenleaf. "You like to sleep, don't you!"

Jeremy Mouse nodded his head. "I'm hungry!" he said. "What are we going to have for breakfast?"

"I don't know," replied Greenleaf. "Someone ate all the muffins yesterday. I wonder who that might be?"

"That must have been me," said Jeremy Mouse with a grin. "They were delicious!" He looked around. "Where are Pine Cone and Pepper Pot?"

"They went out last night and didn't come back," said Greenleaf.

Jeremy Mouse nodded. He was used to gnomes going off at night. Then he threw his arms into the air: "But they had the traveling biscuits!" he moaned. "Now I'm going to be really hungry!"

"I'm sure we can find nuts and seeds," said Tiptoes. "Let's go."

Down the tree they climbed and sailed away in the leaf boat. As they passed out of the grove Greenleaf turned and looked back. "Goodbye trees of the Lost Lagoon!" he waved.

"Goodbye Lost Lagoon! Goodbye!" called Tiptoes and Jeremy Mouse.

Back along the shallow channel they sailed. Not a cloud was in sight and the sun had the blue sky all to itself. Dozens of redwing blackbirds were flying about over their heads and calling to each other. After a while Greenleaf spied a clump of spring bulrushes and stopped the boat.

"Climb up a stalk," he said to Jeremy Mouse. "You can eat bulrush heads when they're young and fresh."

So Jeremy Mouse clambered up a stalk. It was smooth and he kept slipping backwards, but at last he reached the top and started nibbling.

"Mmmm, they're delicious," he called to Tiptoes and Greenleaf. "You should try some," but they shook their heads.

A goldfinch landed on a neighboring bulrush. The bulrush nodded its head up and down and the finch had to flap its wings to keep its balance.

"Chirp! Chirp!" said the goldfinch, its golden feathers shining brightly. "What kind of bird are you? Where are your wings? And that tail of yours is much too skinny for flying."

"I'm not a bird," answered Jeremy Mouse. "I'm a mouse!" The goldfinch looked at him carefully.

"Bulrushes are for birds," said the goldfinch at last. "If you're not careful you'll fall into the water."

"No, I won't," said Jeremy Mouse proudly. "I'm a good climber."

Just then two blackbirds came flying by. One was chasing the other and both were squawking loudly. Round and round in circles they flew over Jeremy Mouse's head. He had to turn round and round too because he was afraid they'd land on his bulrush. Soon he began to feel dizzy.

"Oh, I feel dizzy!" he moaned, staggering about.

"Stop spinning!" shouted Greenleaf.

"Hang on!" shouted Tiptoes.

"I can't," groaned Jeremy Mouse, flailing about and trying to keep his balance. "My legs are all wobbly … and my knees are like jelly … and … and," and off the bulrush he fell.

"Told you so! Told you so!" chirped the goldfinch, gleefully flapping his wings.

"Ker–splash!" went Jeremy Mouse into the water and disappeared underneath the waves.

A moment later up he came, spluttering and gasping for air. The water was cold! Greenleaf and Tiptoes grabbed him by the scruff of the neck and hauled him back into the boat. They were trying not to laugh.

"Let's find a sunny place to dry your fur," said Greenleaf, and off they sailed.

# 41

## *From Bug Ugly to Fly Beautiful*

Jeremy Mouse sat in the sunshine close to the water's edge. Greenleaf had found an island to land on, and Tiptoes had dried his fur with moss. Now he felt warm again. Tiptoes had brought him grass seeds too, and he munched on them happily.

After a while Jeremy Mouse noticed an insect leave the water and climb the stem of an old reed. It was dark brown, with six legs and a big head—it wasn't very pretty. About halfway up the reed it stopped, and making sure its legs firmly grasped the stem, became as still as still can be.

"What's that bug doing?" thought Jeremy Mouse. "He looks like he belongs underwater, and here he is sunbathing!"

He watched carefully. After a while he noticed that the insect's head and back were splitting open.

"Tiptoes! Come here!" he called. "What's happening? This bug is splitting open!"

Tiptoes came over and sat next to him. "Just watch," she said. "You'll soon find out what happens."

Bit by bit the insect pulled its head and chest out of its old skin; then, one by one, its six legs. The old brown legs still clung firmly onto the reed, but his new legs were pale and soft. They also grabbed onto the reed stalk.

The bug sat still for a long time, his tail inside the old skin—this kept him firmly in place. Now and then he moved his legs to test them, and they quickly darkened and became harder. All at once, the insect pulled its tail out of its old skin.

"Look at that!" cried Jeremy Mouse, tugging on Tiptoes' sleeve. "He crawled out of his old skin—but he doesn't look the same at all. Now he's got bigger eyes, and his skin is glowing with beautiful colors!"

Tiptoes smiled, but didn't say a word. Greenleaf came over and watched as well.

The insect's tail grew longer and longer. On each side of his body were two whitish clumps that looked like crumpled leaves. These grew too, and slowly flattened out into delicate petals. They glistened and shone in the sunlight. Jeremy Mouse saw that they were wings.

"It's a dragonfly!" he exclaimed. "The ugly bug became a dragonfly!"

"That's right," said Tiptoes. "That's how dragonflies are born."

"It's a miracle!" cried Jeremy Mouse in astonishment. He was so excited.

As the dragonfly clung to the stalk, its tail and wings finished growing. Jeremy Mouse could hardly believe how much it had changed. Now and then it gently fluttered its wings.

"See," said Tiptoes, "he's drying his wings. They have to be completely firm before he flies."

Just then another dragonfly landed on the reed.

"Quick! Listen carefully!" said Greenleaf, and they all leaned closer. This is what they heard.

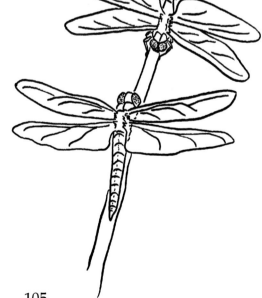

# 42

## The Frog and the Dragonfly

"Dear New Brother Dragonfly," said the old dragonfly, "you have just come out of the water into the light and air. In the water there were many dangers; things like fish and eels who were fond of eating you for breakfast and lunch—even just for a snack! Now you have changed into a colorful being who will live and fly for a short while in the wind and sunshine.

It is much safer in the air, Dear Brother. We are the best flyers in the whole world and we have been on the earth for thousands and thousands of years. But we also have to be wise and use our eyes properly. Listen well to the tale I have to tell you and do not forget it."

"Once there was a dragonfly who lived beside a lake high in the mountains. He flitted from bulrush to bulrush, and zipped after mosquitoes. He snapped them out of the air so quickly that no one could ever quite see what he was doing.

One day, as he was flying across the water, his beautiful wings glistening like rainbows, he came across a frog.

'Ribbit!' said the frog. 'Come here, Mr. Dragonfly. I would like to have a better look at you.'

But the dragonfly was clever. In fact, he was so clever that his eyes were made up of hundreds of eyes all put together on the top of his head. And each one of those eyes said to him: 'That frog wants to eat me!'

So he landed on top of a bulrush where the frog could not get to him, and said, 'Yes, Mr. Frog, I am close enough for you. What do you want?'

'Ribbit! Ribbit!' croaked the frog, 'I think you should come closer because my eyes are not very good.'

So the dragonfly came a little closer. He flitted to a flower floating on the water—but not close enough for the frog to grab him with his mouth.

'Yes, Mr. Frog, what do you want?' he asked.

'Oh, Mr. Dragonfly,' said the frog, 'I have an itch on the end of my nose and my legs aren't long enough to reach it. But your legs are scratchy—they will be able to scratch my itchiness much better that I ever could.'

The dragonfly found this quite funny. He thought, 'That frog wants to eat me! I am sure that frog wants to eat me!' So he flew behind the frog and landed on his back.

The frog could feel the dragonfly crawling on his back, but he could not turn around to grab him. 'Oh, Mr. Dragonfly,' he said, 'you have to come closer to my nose. In fact, my lips are getting very itchy—please come closer.'

So the dragonfly went and sat between the frog's eyes.

Now, the frog knew that the dragonfly had far, far more eyes than he. So he said, 'Oh, Mr. Dragonfly, you are surely much, much more wise than I am. You have so many eyes that you can see the whole world!'

And the dragonfly replied, 'Of course I can see the whole world. I have so many eyes that I am the wisest of all flies!'

'Well,' said the frog, 'I have a little tickle in the bottom of my throat—what is happening there?'

So the dragonfly looked, and looked, and looked … and Snap! the frog ate him up.

"Now you see, Dear New Brother Dragonfly, we have to be careful and far more wise than clever. That's how we stay out of trouble."

Then the old dragonfly lifted lightly off the reed, and the new dragonfly fluttered its wings and followed. Away they flew, zipping this way and that over the water and shimmering in the sunlight.

# 43

# *The Dragonfly Riddles*

Tiptoes left Jeremy Mouse and Greenleaf on the island and skimmed over the marshy land beside Running River. Hundreds of dragonflies zigzagged in the sunshine. Tiptoes liked dragonflies. They looked fierce, but the colors on their wings glistened so brightly. She'd liked the story that the wise old dragonfly had told his younger brother and wondered if another dragonfly would tell her a tale. She spotted one sitting on an old fence post and landed next to it.

"Good day, Master Dragonfly," said Tiptoes politely as she landed beside him. "May your wings catch the wind wisely." Tiptoes knew the proper way to greet unknown dragonflies.

"Thank you, and good day to you too, Mistress Fairy," replied the dragonfly, courteously bobbing his wings up and down. He had never met Tiptoes, but he knew who she was. "May your wings catch the wind wisely too, and may mosquitoes forever be at your mouth."

Tiptoes didn't like to eat mosquitoes for breakfast, lunch and dinner like dragonflies do, but she smiled and made a little curtsy anyway.

"Will you tell me a dragonfly tale?" she asked.

"I will if you answer three of my riddles," replied the dragonfly, looking at her intently.

Tiptoes nodded her head up and down. She knew that dragonflies loved to make up riddles. "Yes," she said. "I'll try."

The dragonfly rubbed his front legs together and thought for a minute.

Then he said:

> *Wind beater,*
> *Mozzie eater!*
> *Side slipper,*
> *Helicopter!*
> *Buzzy guzzler,*
> *Fairy puzzler!*
> ***Who am I?"***

"That's too easy," laughed Tiptoes. "It's you! A dragonfly!"

"Hmm," said the dragonfly to himself, rubbing his wings together and making a dry, crackling sound. "Here's a harder one."

> *"Wave maker,*
> *Leaf shaker!*
> *Branch bender,*
> *Storm sender!*
> *Fire fanner,*
> *Makes a banner*
> *Whirl!*
> ***Who am I?"***

"That's easy too" cried Tiptoes happily. "The wind!"

"You're much too clever," said the dragonfly, rubbing his wings together again. "Here's one that's much harder."

> *"Humans know them,*
> *Beasts dream them,*
> *Plants live them,*
> *Stones sleep them all unknown —*
> ***Who am I?"***

Tiptoes scratched her head. "Humans know them ... and beasts dream them ... what could that be? This one is definitely harder."

"Colors!" she cried. "It must be colors!"

"Well, colors could almost be the answer," said the dragonfly, "but it isn't. Try again."

Tiptoes bit her lip and twirled her hair. "What could this be?" she wondered.

"I'll give you another clue," said the dragonfly, enjoying himself.

> *"They swim all around us*
> *Like fish in the seas;*
> *As huge as elephants,*
> *As small as fleas.*
> *Some taste like honey,*
> *Some sting like bees,*
> *Some close doors,*
> *Some hold keys!*
> **Who am I?"**

"How can something be big and small at the same time," wondered Tiptoes. "And some are nasty, and others nice ... this riddle is hard!"

The dragonfly flitted quickly into the air and down again onto the fence post. He was getting excited. Imagine, beating Tiptoes Lightly at riddles! Then he'd have something to boast about to all his buddies!

"Give me one more clue," begged Tiptoes in her sweetest voice.

"Okay," laughed the dragonfly. "Here's your last clue."

*"Harmless as hedgehogs,*
*Curled in a ball;*
*Dangerous as dragons,*
*Fire and all!*
*Some last a day,*
*And some last forever,*
*Lots can be dumb,*
*But some are real clever.*
**Who am I?"**

"Ideas!" cried Tiptoes suddenly. "Ideas and thoughts! That's the answer to your riddle!"

"Yes," said the dragonfly, "you are right. But I did have to give you three clues!"

"You did, indeed," agreed Tiptoes, "but I guessed the riddle and now you have to tell me a story."

"That I will," said the dragonfly. "What kind of tale do you want, Tiptoes Lightly? A silly dragonfly tale, or a sad dragonfly tale?"

"It's far too sunny and cheerful this morning for a sad story," said Tiptoes. "It'll have to be the silly one."

This is the story the dragonfly told her.

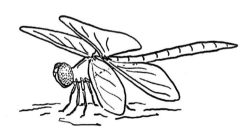

# 44

## *The Show-Off Dragonfly and what happened to Him*

Once there was a dragonfly. He zoomed and zipped around like a sports car, flashing fancy colors and doing loop-de-loops in front of a flitter of damselflies—and these damsels were not impressed.

"Ha!" they snickered to each other in the way only damselflies can snicker when they are being nasty. "He thinks he's so fancy and flashy, doing his loop-de-loops and nincompoops, but he's just a showoff!" And they all turned their pretty tails towards him and flew away.

Well, the dragonfly was not going to have that! Off he flew after the damsels as quick as a wink.

Zzzzoom! he whizzed past them faster than a speeding bullet. "Wheee! Look at me!" he called, as he twisted and spun around in a fancy barrel roll. Then, to really show off, he flew upside down, popped chewing gum into his mouth, put two legs lazily behind his head, scratched his tummy with two other legs, and the last two cleaned wax out of his ears. All this he did at once!

Then the hard-nosed damsels felt their hearts go pitter-patter and begin to melt. Imagine doing all those wonderful things and flying upside down at the same time!

But hardly had their silly hearts begun to soften, when SPLAT, the dragonfly crashed into a tree.

"Ah!" cried one damselfly.

"Oh!" cried the other.

"Eeek!" cried the rest, and they all rushed to his side … but the poor dragonfly was dead, the wad of chewing gum hanging out of his mouth.

"Oh, he was the best!" sobbed one damselfly.

"The most handsome!" moaned the other.

"So daring! So clever!" sighed the rest, and they all wept so much for their fallen hero that their pitter-patter hearts broke in two, and out rushed huge bubbles of hot air which blew away in the wind."

"And that," said the dragonfly, "is the end of a tale for the price of a riddle," and off he flew over Running River, zipping this way and that and snapping mosquitoes out of the air.

113

# 45

## *Leaving and Leaves*

It was after midday and Tiptoes, Jeremy Mouse and Greenleaf the Sailor were drifting down Running River. They were keeping a sharp eye out for Pine Cone and Pepper Pot as the bluffs loomed closer.

"The gnomes should be around here somewhere," said Tiptoes. "I know there's a doorway to a silver cave hereabouts."

She was right. They found the gnomes snoozing on a rock directly below the Oh-Oh! Tree.

"Pine Cone! Pepper Pot!" called Jeremy Mouse. "Wake up! We're here!"

The gnomes sat up and waved merrily. Greenleaf sailed the boat to the shore and they clambered in. Slowly the afternoon passed. Greenleaf let Running River carry his little boat along on its winding, meandering way. The sky was blue, the sun was yellow, and all the meadows and fields were decked out in fresh spring green.

A peach orchard in bloom drifted past, with thousands of peach blossom petals fluttering in the gentle breeze. The breeze ruffled Jeremy Mouse's fur and played with Tiptoes' golden hair. Tiptoes was getting restless. She had been sitting in the boat for a long time and the wind was calling to her. She wanted to fly. She opened her wings and leapt lightly into the air.

"Hey!" called Jeremy Mouse after her. "Where are you going?"

But Tiptoes didn't reply—she was already higher than the trees.

"I think the wind is calling to her," said Pine Cone. "She wants to fly."

114

Jeremy Mouse nodded understandingly and lay down in the boat. He looked up and watched the overhanging branches passing by. Whenever the breeze blew the branches dipped and the leaves shimmered.

"Leaves are such lovely creatures," said Jeremy Mouse dreamily. "I like their shapes and the way they turn to the light."

"I love leaves too," agreed Greenleaf, looking up at the tress.

"That's why you're called Greenleaf," said Jeremy Mouse with a mischievous grin. "And not Lizard-Liker, or Puddle-Jumper or something like that."

Greenleaf chuckled and nodded his head. "I don't think I'd like to be called Lizard-Liker," he said. "That'd be horrible—even though I do like lizards!"

Jeremy Mouse and Greenleaf looked at the leaves some more.

"I wonder what the life of a leaf is like?" said Jeremy Mouse at last.

"I can tell you a tiny tale that a leaf once told me," offered Greenleaf. "Then you'll know what it's like to be a leaf."

"What's it called?" asked Jeremy Mouse, sitting up.

"It's called, '*The Life of a Leaf*', said Greenleaf, with a little laugh. "What else?"

115

# 46

## *The Life of a Leaf*

Once upon a time there lived a leaf. It was a green leaf, as green as a green leaf can be. It loved the sun, and the leaf lay itself out flat so the sun could shine down upon it with its golden rays. And the leaf had rays too, five big ones, just like the sun, for it grew upon a maple tree.

This leaf had been born in springtime, growing quickly, and very, very quietly, on the end of a branch high above the ground. It waved in the wind and fluttered in the breeze. How the leaf loved to tremble when it was stroked by the breeze!

All summer long the leaf stayed on the tree, listening to the birds, and letting the rain wash it clean and make it glisten. Then autumn came. The days grew shorter, and the nights much longer and cooler. One night, when the moon was waxing, Jack Frost flew down from the mountains and covered the leaf with ice crystals.

'That makes me feel chilly,' said the leaf to itself. 'I shall have to put on my frost coat,' and the next day he donned his yellow jacket.

'This shall keep me warm,' he said to himself.

But Jack Frost came back again that very night and covered the leaf with frost.

'I shall put on a warmer coat,' said the leaf, and turned himself bright orange.

'Oh, how pretty I look in my orange jacket!' he declared, very proud of himself.

But two nights later, when the moon was full, Jack Frost returned, glistening and crackling in the moonlight. He breathed white frost over the ground, on the trees, and on all the leaves. He made pools of water stand as still as ice, and people had to blow on their fingers and nails.

So the leaf put on his last and warmest coat—a bright red one. Now he really looked festive.

'Oh, how festive I am!' exclaimed the leaf to himself. 'I have the warmest, reddest jacket of all the leaves in the forest! I burn with fire and I shall chase Jack Frost away!'

But Jack Frost did not stay away. Down he flew over the land and all that night the tree's roots called out: 'Oh, leaf! Beautiful leaf! Cover me up and keep me warm or I shall freeze!'

The next morning, just as the sun was rising, the leaf let go of his branch. For a little while he fluttered like a red bird flying in the air. Then he lay on the ground. Hundreds and thousands of his brothers and sisters let go of their branches too. Whole flocks of them flew down to the earth to keep the roots warm. And they did keep the roots warm—all winter long. Then Jack Frost could not freeze the roots and the tree felt safe from harm.

In the spring, when the sun finally chased Jack Frost away, the leaf had turned brown—just like the earth. Soon he broke into little pieces and the red worms carried his body down to the hungry tree roots. This made the tree strong, and it put forth new green leaves, as green as green leaves can be. And when the breeze came blowing by, all the leaves fluttered and trembled to her touch."

"Which maple leaf told you that story?" asked Jeremy Mouse.

"A leaf from the maple tree growing close to Farmer John's house," said Greenleaf. "In springtime its leaves are freshest green, and in fall they are so colorful it dazzles 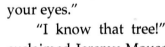 your eyes."

"I know that tree!" exclaimed Jeremy Mouse. "I saw it last autumn— it was gorgeous!" and he lay back in the boat again and looked up at all the leaves waving in the wind.

# 47

## *Tom finds Tiptoes' House*

Tiptoes flew over Farmer John's fields. His orchards were bursting with white almond and pink cherry blossoms fluttering in the breeze. She flew over his house and saw June Berry playing on the swing under the mulberry tree. Then she headed towards her oak tree. She wanted to see how her acorn house was doing. So much had happened that it felt like ages since she'd left, even though it had only been yesterday.

As she came closer she saw someone high in the branches. She knew at once who it was.

"Hello, Tom," she said, landing on a branch next to him. "Looking for something?"

Tom Nutcracker grinned and nodded.

"Your house," he admitted. "I want to see it for myself. My dad's sure he spotted it a couple of days ago."

"He did," said Tiptoes. "Come, I'll show you," and she led Tom upwards to the highest branch. Just when Tom thought the branches were too slim to stand on, he saw it: a single acorn dangling by its stem.

Tom was astonished. Tiptoes' house was so small, yet it had two windows and a door with a knocker. Tiptoes flew to the door and went in. Then she opened a window and popped her head out.

"See!" she said, flinging out her arms in a gesture of joy. "My house!"

Tom peered in the window. He spied a tiny round table and three finely made chairs, their seats woven from spider's silk.

"Those are beautiful!" Tom exclaimed.

"Pine Cone and Pepper Pot made them for my birthday," said Tiptoes proudly. "They had a hard time getting them all the way up here."

Tom looked in the other window. It was Tiptoes' bedroom. She had a bed made from two downy feathers; one to lie on and one to cover her up.

"Those feathers are from Lucy the Goose," said Tiptoes. "She gave them to me before she flew south for the winter. They keep me cozy."

Tom smiled. He couldn't believe how perfect her house was. She even had curtains on the windows.

After Tom had a good look Tiptoes said: "I think your father wants to have a word with you. He'd like to know where you went last night."

Tom looked at Tiptoes in surprise. How did she know he'd been to the Lost Lagoon? And how did his dad know about it as well? He'd gotten up early and taken the blanket off Chiron and put it back in the barn. He certainly wasn't at all sure what he'd say to his father about his midnight adventure.

"How do you know my dad wants to see me," asked Tom nervously.

"That's easy," said Tiptoes, pointing to the ground. "He's standing underneath the tree and waiting for you to climb down!"

# 48

# *Home Again*

The sun was low in the sky when Tiptoes returned and landed in the boat.

"We're almost back at Greenleaf's willow tree," she said. "I just flew over it."

"Where did you go?" asked Jeremy Mouse.

"Here and there and in the air," replied Tiptoes Lightly. "I flew over Farmer John's, then I went back to our oak tree. I found Tom Nutcracker in the branches looking for my house."

"Did you show it to him?" asked Pine Cone.

"I did," said Tiptoes, nodding her head. "Then his father turned up looking for him."

"Oh-oh!" gasped Pepper Pot, looking concerned—Greenleaf had told the gnomes all about Tom's full-moon adventure. "Did he get into trouble?"

"A bit," said Tiptoes. "But he did the right thing by rubbing Chiron down and putting a horse blanket on. That saved him!"

"How did his dad find out about his adventures?" asked Pine Cone.

"That was easy!" said Tiptoes. "He saw Tom's footprints going towards the barn in the morning dew. He checked Chiron's stall and found that the horse blanket was damp. That told him Tom had been out riding at night."

Greenleaf stood up by the prow and sang a homecoming song. His voice sounded as clear as a bell over the waters of Running River, and his leaf boat sprang to life and glided quickly forwards.

The air was cool and the waning moon rising over the Snowy Mountains as they came around the last bend in the river and saw Greenleaf's willow tree waiting patiently for them.

"Goodbye, Greenleaf," called Tiptoes and Jeremy Mouse as they headed back home. "Thank you for taking us to the Lost Lagoon."

"You're welcome," answered Greenleaf.

"Goodbye, Tiptoes and Jeremy Mouse," called Pine Cone and Pepper Pot, waving their red hats. The gnomes had decided to stay at Greenleaf's house for the night

Tiptoes and Jeremy Mouse walked home across the meadows to their great oak tree. It stood proudly on its knoll overlooking Running River. Behind it in the west the setting sun painted the sky red and pink and orange.

"Goodnight," called Tiptoes as Jeremy Mouse went into his house underneath the roots of the oak tree.

"Goodnight, Tiptoes," answered Jeremy Mouse with a yawn. He was ready for bed.

Tiptoes spread her wings and flew lightly into the air. Turning towards the sun she raised her hands, and said:

> *"Thank you, Sun,*
> *O Being so bright,*
> *For sending love*
> *In rays as light."*

And turning towards the rising moon she called:

> *"Thank you, Moon,*
> *O mistress of night,*
> *For pearls so pure*
> *On my necklace bright."*

Then into her house Tiptoes flew and lay down on her soft feather bed. A gentle breeze sprung up and rocked her acorn house back and forth. She listened to the voice of the wind for a little while, then closed her eyes and fell fast sleep.

121

**49**

# Adam makes a Pot for Evening Star

Tom Nutcracker felt lucky. He only had to clean out Chiron's stall for a week. His dad hadn't been too angry. In fact, Tom sensed that he was secretly proud of his son's adventure.

After supper Farmer John gathered his children for their bedtime story. Lucy joined them too, as he always did. He didn't understand the stories, but he liked the sound of his master's voice. Farmer John placed 'The Adam Tales' on his lap and opened it.

"Is this the last chapter of the book?" asked June Berry.

"Yes," said Farmer John. "It's called: *Adam makes a Pot for Evening Star*," and he began to read.

"Adam had a new body made of clay. He also had new eyes and saw the world as a human being. He looked with great wonder at many things: antelope and deer, wildebeest and tigers, even whales in the great ocean. He beheld the mountains, the rivers, the hills and plains as if they had never been seen before, and was amazed.

Adam also saw with spirit eyes, and always knew when his angel friends visited him. Often his closest friend came too. Adam thought she was the most beautiful being he had ever looked upon. And she was, indeed, beautiful. They spent many happy hours walking in the mountains or talking together beside the river. He told her of all the things he saw with his new eyes and what it was like to live on the earth, and she would bring news from all the other angels and stars.

But slowly, as the years went by, Adam's spirit eyes began to dim. His friend became harder to see, and even though he often dreamed of her, less and less was he able to meet her in the daytime. Gradually, the first man on earth found himself alone. He had never felt alone before—he did not even know how to name his feeling— but in his heart he knew, and it weighed heavily upon him.

Many times in the early evening Adam climbed a hill and looked for the evening star that shone so brightly in the East. He knew that his closest friend lived there and that they shared the same name. Then he felt her presence, and for a little while was happy again. But the evening star was a wandering star and not always in the sky. Then Adam felt more alone than ever and began to despair.

One night he had a dream. In his dream Evening Star came to him, and said: 'I miss you too, dear friend. I would like to come to the earth and be with you. But you must make me a vessel of finest clay and put the best three animals you can find into the pot. Then I will jump into the pot just like you, and say the magic word.'

In the morning Adam awoke and journeyed back to the river he had visited many years before. So much time had passed that the river no longer flowed in its old bed, but the soft, silky clay on its banks was as fine as ever—even finer perhaps.

'This is the best clay for my friend,' he said to himself, and dug it up to make a pot. All day he labored and in the evening the pot was ready. He built a large fire, and the flames filled the night that had gathered around him. But, as he was putting the pot into the fire, Evening Star spoke from out of the flames:

'You have made a beautiful pot, dear friend,' she said, 'but its shape is the same as yours. I am not you, and you are not me. You must make a different pot.'

So the next day Adam dug fresh clay and fashioned a new pot. This one was much finer, with graceful forms and shapes. All day he worked, and as he worked he thought of nothing other than his friend. Just as day ended he finished, and again he collected wood and built a large fire. As the flames danced in the darkness he picked up the pot and placed it gently inside. Then the evening star rose in the heavens, and the moon shed her beautiful light over the landscape.

In the morning Adam took the pot out of the ashes. He brushed it off and looked at it carefully. It was a perfect pot for his friend, with never a flaw or wrinkle to be seen. 'I shall not leave this pot by the riverbank,' he thought to himself. 'I never did find out who kept moving my pot and I do not want to take any chances.' So he put the pot under his arm and went to look for the best animals.

Over valleys and hills he traveled till he came to a wide grassland prairie. There he saw a mighty bull standing tall and proud. 'That is a good animal for my Evening Star,' he declared. 'He is every bit as fine as the bull I chose.'

But Evening Star appeared over the bull, and said: 'No, dear friend, this is not who I really am. You must search again.'

So off Adam went across the grassy plain, seeking and searching. At last he spotted a deer delicately eating the fresh grass.

'That is a good animal for my friend,' he said, and went towards it. But the deer flicked her tail at him and leapt away. Instantly Adam took off after her and all day long they ran across the plain. But in the evening she was still far ahead of him.

Adam was in despair. 'What am I to do?' he cried. 'That is the best and finest animal for my friend.'

He thought for a while. When the evening star rose in the sky he began to sing. Softly and gently he sang until the deer turned towards him and listened. Slowly she approached. She had never heard such a wonderful voice, so kind and gentle, and at last she let Adam reach out and stroke her. Then he said:

> 'Into the pot for Evening Star,
> It won't be long till she's not far,'

and the deer willingly leapt into the pot.

All day and all night Adam wandered till he came to a forest. There he met a fierce lion with proud head and majestic mane. 'That beast is every bit as fine as the one that beats in my breast,' he thought. But Evening Star appeared over the lion, and said: 'Dear friend, that beast is fine indeed, but not for me. You must look again.'

This time Adam didn't have far to look. Just then, a lioness appeared out of the brush. She was smooth and sleek and growled quietly … or was she purring? … Adam wasn't sure!

'That is the animal for my Evening Star,' he thought, and went towards the lioness. But she was wild; she hissed and spat at him and bared her claws. Quietly Adam began to sing; deep into the night Adam sang, and when the evening star was highest in the heavens the lioness turned, walked towards him and freely leapt into the pot.

Far Adam traveled, over rock and over scree, till he came to a mountain. He looked up at its craggy heights and saw golden eagles soaring and circling in the air over its summit. 'Those are fine birds indeed, so golden and bright,' he thought. 'They would be perfect for my friend.'

He climbed the steep sides of the mountain and scaled its cliffs until he came to the peak. As he stood on the highest rock one bird swooped low over his head and screeched loudly. He saw the fierce glint in its eye, its merciless talons and sharp beak, and knew in his heart that this was not the right bird for his friend. Evening Star was far more gentle, and her voice soft and kind.

So Adam kept wandering, looking carefully at all the birds and listening to their song. He saw bright parrots and shimmering hummingbirds that drank from flowers. He saw elegant swans flying in the air, and heard goldfinches and red-winged blackbirds singing in the sunlight. All were beautiful, but none were right for his friend.

Adam began to lose heart, but one evening he heard a gentle cooing coming from a nearby wood. He searched around and found a white dove sitting in an olive tree overhanging a clear, freshwater spring. Adam saw the light of his friend shining around the dove, and in the evening sky her bright star was rising.

Adam held the pot high in the air and the dove swooped down and landed on its rim. Adam sang:

> 'Into the pot for Evening Star,
> It won't be long till she's not far,'

and into the pot the dove flew.

Then Adam filled the pot with living water from the spring, held it towards the bright evening star, and his dearest friend leapt inside. She called the magic word, and instantly the pot trembled. It quivered and shook and shifted shape in Adam's hands. Soon a woman's form appeared. She had silky skin and beautiful eyes that sparkled like stars. Her hands were wonderfully wrought too, with long, sensitive fingers and a gentle touch.

At last the first woman on earth was complete. Evening Star became Adam's earthly companion, and the first mother of all human beings. For long ages her proper name was remembered, but slowly it changed and shortened. Then the first woman became known as Eve."

# 50

## *Farmer John wonders*

Farmer John turned the page, but that was the end of the story. He closed the book and looked at the back cover. It said nothing about any more Adam Tales, but he decided to find out if the stories continued in another book.

After Tom Nutcracker and June Berry were in bed, Farmer John stood on his front porch. The waning moon was rising over the forest and the western sky still glowed dimly from the setting sun. A gentle breeze wafted by. It carried the sounds of the frogs singing in Running River.

"I wonder what those frogs have so much to sing about?" he mused. "It's almost as if they're singing about something lost and mysterious."

Far away, Farmer John could see the Great Oak Tree sitting on its knoll. He'd found Tom high up in the tree that afternoon, talking to the acorn he'd spotted earlier—or at least so it seemed.

"An acorn couldn't possibly be a fairy's house," he said, scratching his head.

But Farmer John wasn't sure. After all, he had seen this acorn before. In fact, now that he thought about it, he'd seen it for years on the very same branch. And no matter how strongly the wind blew the acorn always stayed put.

"Perhaps I'll climb up there some day," he said to himself. "Well ... maybe not. I'm much too heavy to climb such thin branches. And besides, there really couldn't be a fairy house inside an acorn ... could there?"

Then, still scratching his head, Farmer John went back inside the house and closed the door.

### The End

# Author's Note
## Second Edition

**Dear 'Old' Readers:** It's taken a while to get *The Lost Lagoon* out. A number of you contacted me, asking for another Tiptoes book and I did respond by writing the story ... but there things got stuck. The illustrations just were not getting done. I was busy with my adult students and all the demands of a eurythmy* training. Then, the lead group having graduated, I found myself with the time to tackle the illustrations and the cover. Now it is done and I am pleased. So thank you to all the readers who encouraged me to keep writing. I recently did a count of books sold and, collectively, the Tiptoes books have passed the 15,500 mark. Yea for Tiptoes! I know that this is small beans compared to the big guns of publishing, but to me this means that thousands of children have heard her stories and this warms my heart.

I'd like to thank those who gifted me with drawings made by their children, those who have taken a moment to let me know that your children love these tales, and those who have spent time writing reviews. Thank you also to the many teachers who have told me that these tales are part of their lessons, have been 'translated' into class plays, are used as readers, or are read to the children simply for pleasure.

**Dear New Readers:** Those new to Tiptoes Lightly will perhaps not realize that she is real. Tiptoes first became part of my kindergarten lessons at the Monadnock Waldorf School in Keene, New Hampshire, and consequently followed me to the Camellia Waldorf School in Sacramento, California. Her presence in my eurythmy lessons when one of her stories was 'up', or when I am writing about her, is palpable. There is a definite shift of mood and the stories just flow. Sometimes she sits on my shoulder (the left one) or curls herself up in my heart when she wants to rest and dream.

* Eurythmy is an art of movement and gesture using speech and music as its basis. It lends itself to vivid nature and spirit-filled stories.

Northern California is where the tales, in a loose way, are set. Here the Sacramento and American rivers wend their way to the Pacific ocean from the snowcapped Sierra Nevada mountains. And in the village of Fair Oaks there really is an Oh-Oh! Tree hanging over the bluffs beside the American river. I have even gone looking for the Lost Lagoon—unfortunately the flood waters had receded and it was not to be found! I'll try again if the river spills its banks next spring.

If you'd like to read more books about Tiptoes and company (plus other books, too) please see the list on the next page. Sample stories from all the books and a number of stand-alone tales (even a play) are on my website: **www.tiptoes-lightly.net**. You will also find children's art inspired by Tiptoes and crew, crafts and art from adult readers, and photographs of yours truly doing puppet shows.

All the best,
Reg Down, Sacramento, California
Michaelmas, 2011

Rate it: if you enjoyed this book,
please, next time you're on Amazon,
give it a couple of words + as many stars as
your enjoyment.
The biggest challenge as a self-published author
is promotion, and what people see on Amazon
definitely makes a difference.
~ Thank you ~

More books by Reg Down

# The Tales of Tiptoes Lightly
*(The Tales of Tiptoes Lightly is being translated
into Spanish and German too!)*

# The Festival of Stones

# Big-Stamp Two-Toes the Barefoot Giant

# The Magic Knot ~ and other tangles!

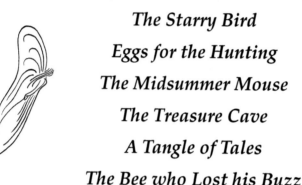

# The Starry Bird

# Eggs for the Hunting

# The Midsummer Mouse

# The Treasure Cave

# A Tangle of Tales

# The Bee who Lost his Buzz

# The Cricket and the Shepherd Boy
*(In Spanish too!)*

# The Darkling Beasts

# The Adventures of Jane: the cat who was a dog

# The Fetching of Spring
*A novel*

# Color and Gesture
*An Exploration of the Inner Life of Color*

# Leaving Room for the Angels
*Eurythmy and the Art of Teaching*
*(AWSNA Publications)*

3 1269 01852 0118

9 781453 801963